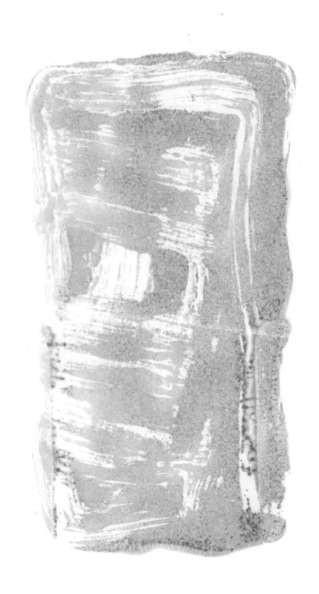

TALL TALES

from the

HIGH HILLS

ELLIS CREDLE

TALL TALES

from the

HIGH HILLS

AND OTHER STORIES

ILLUSTRATED BY RICHARD BENNETT

THOMAS NELSON & SONS

Edinburgh   NEW YORK   *Toronto*

Books by Ellis Credle

TALL TALES FROM THE HIGH HILLS
BIG DOIN'S ON RAZORBACK RIDGE
DOWN, DOWN THE MOUNTAIN
ADVENTURES OF TITTLETOM
JOHNNY AND HIS MULE

Grateful acknowledgment for permission to reprint stories is made to: THE
CANADIAN RED CROSS JUNIOR for *A Tall Turnip, The Self-Kicking Machine,*
and *Old Plott;* AMERICAN JUNIOR RED CROSS JOURNAL for *The Perambulat-
in' Pumpkin;* AMERICAN JUNIOR RED CROSS NEWS for *Surprise for the Black
Bull;* STORY PARADE for *The Bear and the Wildcat, The Blizzard of '98,
The Goat that Went to School, Janey's Shoes, The Pudding that Broke up
the Preaching,* and *The Short Horse.*

TO

My Mother

Sixth Printing, January 1966

© *1957, by Ellis Credle*

Library of Congress Catalog Card Number: 57-10019

PRINTED IN THE UNITED STATES OF AMERICA

How the Tall Tales Grew

When we moved to the small community in the Blue Ridge Mountains, we took a little house in the bottomlands, between two great mountains. From our front porch we could see, far up on the mountainside, a tiny cabin like the ones the early settlers must have built. In the distance it looked like a toy cabin with smoke rising from its chimney. In lowering weather, it was invisible for the clouds hung below it and hid it from sight. We wondered who lived there, in that lonely and hard-to-reach spot. One day we asked the storekeeper at the crossroads.

"Oh, that cabin belongs to Hank Huggins," was the reply. "I'd give him a wide berth if I was you. He's just an old liar. He'll even tell a whopper when the truth would do as well."

We forgot about Hank Huggins. My husband and I had come to the mountains to search for old tales to make a book. We were busy, traipsing around from one old granny to another, trying to find one who remembered some of the stories of her grandmothers' day. But the only tales we tracked down turned out to be some "real pretty stories" the old folks had heard on radio programs.

Then we happened to meet Mr. Huggins in the general store one day. He introduced himself to the "furriners" and in the ensuing conversation we asked how he had come to choose such a lonely site for his home. "You come up sometime and I'll show you," he told us.

Less than a week later we found ourselves climbing the trail to Hank Huggins' cabin. The trees were bright with the gold and russet of autumn, and the climb was so steep that we were winded when we arrived on the heights.

Mr. Huggins and his wife—a quiet little body—greeted us hospitably. He ushered us toward the porch, then, putting a hand on my shoulder, turned and made a gesture toward the mountains.

"There's the reason I live up here!"

He nodded toward the valley spread out below in an opal-blue haze. We could see the tiny houses of the village along the straight ribbon of the highway; the creek was a thread winding among the homesteads.

We went into the cabin. A small fire was burning on the hearth. Mr. Huggins pulled up some rickety ladderback chairs and we sat down, spreading our hands gratefully to the blaze. To make conversation, my husband asked if there were any dangerous animals in the woods.

"Well, not so many now. But in the old days—*whew!*" Hank Huggins whistled and shook his head. "The varmints that used to be up here and the things that used to happen! Why, I recollect one time that a bear and a wildcat—" And the old man launched into a story. From this he progressed to another, and then to a third.

These were probably some of the "whoppers" the storekeeper had mentioned. But we were like people who had stumbled on a gold mine. We felt the excitement of a great discovery. Mr. Huggins was surely a man left over from a way of life now vanished, when people sat around the fire telling tales their grandparents had passed down to them, or making new ones out of half-forgotten lore. We sat entranced.

"However did you come to know so many stories?" I demanded at last.

Hank Huggins gave us a quizzical look. "What is it that has a tongue but can't talk?" Then, seeing our blank expressions: "Shucks, that's the oldest riddle there is. It's a wagon. A wagon's got a tongue but it can't talk. Only my wagon *could*. It heard plenty of tales.

"It was like this. When I was a young fellow, I had a job driving a freight wagon from up here in the hills down to the low country. It was before the railroad was built through the mountains. Well, there used to be a lot of us fellows driving wagons, and we would go together in trains, so as to have help in case somebody got stuck in the mud or broke an axle. Nights we'd camp together in some nice grove. Whilst we were cooking our suppers and after we'd et them, we'd sit around swapping news or telling tales. The tales I've heard around those campfires! Every fellow trying to outdo the next one."

The light outside had changed. It was time for us to go. When we stepped outside, we were amazed to see that the valley down below was dark with blue shadows. Mr. and Mrs. Huggins walked to the gate with us.

"You'll be coming back soon? You won't forget now, will you?"

"We won't forget," I promised.

The tales in this book, the legacies from the wagoners and herders gathered around those long-dead campfires, and the mountain folk around their hearths, are proof that I kept my promise.

ELLIS CREDLE

Contents

The Big Mudhole

"Yes, sir, the world has changed since I was a young'un," declared Hank Huggins. "Everything was different then. We even had different things to worry about. Why, I can recollect when a big mudhole kept mountain folks awake and worrying all night long. They couldn't sleep for thinking of it."

"A mudhole?" His visitor hitched his chair a little closer to the fire which was leaping on the hearth. A cold autumn wind was blowing through the chinks of the small log cabin. "How could a mudhole keep people worrying?"

"If you'd a-seen it, you'd know." Mr. Huggins shook his head. "I reckon I was the only man that ever figured out how to beat that quagmire. I was thinking of it just before you got here. It was the train that put me in mind of it. I was sitting there in the door a-looking down into the valley, watching the engine pulling the cars around the mountains, ducking into tunnels and coming out again, then streaming on around the ledges.

"The railroad hadn't been built up here in the mountains in the days when that mudhole kept everybody worried half to death. You'd be surprised what a difference that made. When folks had to sell anything like a load of apples in the fall, or a wagon full of tobacco, they had to hitch up a team of mules to

9

a wagon and drive down the mountain trails with it to some city in the lowlands. And if they had a drove of hogs or a herd of cattle, those critters had to travel to market on their own feet. Folks had to herd 'em down themselves.

"Roads then weren't what they are today. In some places they were just cow tracks. Sometimes a shallow creek bed was all the track there was, and folks had to drive along it until they came to some passable trail. Down on the flat country it was a little better but even there it wasn't any picnic to travel. It was muddy when it was raining and dusty as all get out in dry weather. Oh, I can tell you, getting your stuff to town in those days was a troublesome business. Folks used to come back with things to tell. And one of the things they told about was that mudhole.

"It was at the foot of a long slope that sort of eased down from the mountains. The road entered the big woods about there. The trees on each side of the road hadn't ever been touched by an ax. They grew in rows on both sides, towering up like black walls, all tangled with vines and bushes. The road was a little cut through this here trackless woods, and the rains rolling down that big slope just seemed to dam up there. The water didn't drain off. The sun never struck through that wall of trees to dry it. It was gloomy in there all the time and got dark a long time before sundown. So all that water stayed and soaked into the ground.

"It sure was a mucky mess! Wagons and buggies cutting through it, horses and mules and critters trampling through, churned it into a heavy black cream. Everybody going down from the mountains got stuck in it and they had a heck of a time getting out. There was a man I knew that rode into that mud on a mule loaded down with sacks of corn. The mule began to mire. The more he floundered to get out the deeper he sank. If that fellow hadn't been pretty quick that mule would have gone out of sight—clean down to China. But the man grabbed the bridle rein and threw it over a limb. He tied it there. Then he reached around and grabbed a-holt of the critter's tail. He scrambled off onto the side of the road, still holding onto that tail. He took a half hitch with it around a sapling and held on. The mule hung there by the head and tail, like a hammock slung between two poles, until a party of wagons came along and the drivers pried the poor beast out with poles.

"There were signs of trouble all around that mudhole—prying poles lying about, baggage that had been thrown out to lighten the load, clothes and shoes that people had taken off and just thrown away after they'd had to get out and flounder through that muck up to their necks.

"The place was as long as from here to there—" Mr. Huggins pointed from the cabin steps to the yard gate. "About half as long as a city block, I reckon. A bottomless trough of mud, a sinkhole that got worse all the time.

"Folks starting a trip began studying about that mudhole before they left home, a-wondering if they'd get through it, hoping there hadn't been any rain down that way lately to make it worse. They used to travel in parties so as to have help if they began to go down.

"Well, sir, the first few times I had to cross that mudhole I had trouble, I can tell you. One time, coming back from Charleston, away down on the coast, I was loaded down with iron strips that blacksmiths up here in the mountains used for rimming wagon wheels. Those iron strips made a heavy load, and when I got into that mudhole with 'em, the wagon just began to sink clean out of sight. I had to skip out of there in a hurry and cut the mules' harness or they would have been dragged down with the wagon. It was the last I ever saw of that load. It disappeared into the mud; never even made a bubble.

"So, the next time I set off for the lowlands, I naturally began to worry about that mudhole. I had a load of apples in a two-horse wagon. That was heavy enough but, to make matters worse, I had me a passenger. His name was Mel Honeycutt. He was tall—six feet or so—and with it, he was fat. I reckon he weighed three hundred pounds. But he was a lively fellow and quick to get around, even with all that weight. I was wondering for sure how I was going to make it through that mudhole with a heavy load of apples and Mel, a-sitting there in the front of the wagon.

"But I always claimed if you put your mind to it you can think your way out of every kind of difficulty. Well, I put my mind to it, and just like I told you, I thought of a way to get my load over that big quagmire clean as a whistle, without even getting the wheels muddy.

"How did I do it? Well, it took a little figuring, I have to admit. But here's how I did it. In the first place, I had me a

right smart of a big wagon and I loaded it heavy in the back. All those apples were piled up in the rear end. I reckon if I had thrown on one more back there, that wagon would have stood up on its hind wheels like a dog begging for a biscuit.

"Mel and I got into the front seat and we started down the mountain. He'd heard about the mudhole like everybody else and he was a-worrying how we were going to get through it. So when I told him my plan he was glad to promise to help me out. He said he'd do just what I told him to.

"When we got to that incline that led down to the mudhole, I got out and unhitched the mules and tied 'em to a tree. Then I folded the wagon tongue back so I could hold it and steer with it. I got in and sat down and reminded Mel Honeycutt of his part. He was a mite nervous, but willing to try. The wagon had already begun to roll down the hill. Wasn't any trouble to steer it because the wheels naturally stayed in the ruts in the road. It picked up speed as it went down. By the time it got to the bottom, it was whizzing so fast the wind was about cutting our ears off. When I saw that mudhole looming almost under our wheels, I yelled at Mel.

" 'Jump!' I hollered.

"He was ready and he was game. He gave a leap toward the back of the wagon on top of all the apples. It upended the thing just as I'd thought. The back part went down and the front lifted. Well, sir, that wagon sailed right up into the air. The speed we had up took her soaring over that mire just like she was shot outen a cannon. When I saw we'd made it I hollered 'Now!'

"Old Mel scrambled back to the front of the wagon. That made the front end come down again. We lit with the front wheels as neat as you please and rolled a little up the other incline. Then we stopped.

"I got out and put a block under the wheels to keep from

rolling back into the mudhole. Then I walked back along the edge of the road where it was fairly hard and led my mules over. They floundered through all right. We hitched up and went on.

"Too bad there wasn't anybody around to see how we flew over that puddle. Seems like I never could load my wagon just right to do it again, and old Mel took off in a vessel from Charleston and never came back to the mountains. So he wasn't around to bear me out. Folks never would believe it happened. When I told about it they just thought I was lying. But it sure did happen. As sure as I'm a-sitting here, it did!"

The Perambulatin' Pumpkin

Down in Beaverdam Valley the mountain folk had gathered
for the county fair. Mr. Zeke Calloway held up a bulging
pumpkin decorated with the blue ribbon for the first prize,
and grinned triumphantly at his neighbor and rival, Mr.
Hank Huggins.

"Reckon you don't grow pumpkins like that on your side
of the mountain!" he crowed.

"Law me," drawled Hank who had been known on oc-
casion to stretch the truth somewhat. "Law me, that little
bitty thing would look like a peanut beside the pumpkins in
my patch."

"Mighty funny thing you didn't bring any of your monstrous pumpkins to the fair," sniggered Zeke. "Mighty funny."

"Well, now, to tell you the truth I was aiming to bring
one but we had a little accident up in our place this morning.
It broke up my plans somewhat."

"What kind of accident?" asked Zeke suspiciously.

"Well, you see it was this way: My wife had laid off to bring
a pumpkin pie to the fair. She was up early baking the crust,
and soon as it was done she climbed up the mountain to the
field where the pumpkins were a-growing among the corn-
stalks.

"Of course all the pumpkins were too big and too heavy to carry, so she set out to cut a slab out of one, enough to make the filling for her pie.

"Seems she had trouble with that, too. Those pumpkins were so thick through that her arm wasn't long enough to reach into the inside where the juicy part was. But she was bound to get some of the very best part for she meant to take first prize with her pie. So what did she do but hack out a big hole and climb through it right into the center of that pumpkin.

"Now that would have been all right if the field where I planted 'em hadn't been so steep. But you know how it is— sometimes a pumpkin will break off the vine by its own weight and go rolling down the mountain.

"Well, you can just picture what happened when that hefty wife of mine added her weight to the strain already on that vine. Before she knew what was happening, she was tumbling head over heels inside that pumpkin as it rolled out of the cornfield.

"I was in the barn lot hitching up the mule to the wagon when I looked up and saw it coming, a-picking up speed every minute. Before I could gather my wits to think what to do, it had hit the lot fence with a crash that sent the rails flying like matches. It tore through the barnyard, hit my wagon amidships, and sent the wheels flying four ways at once. The chickens and ducks ran squawking for their lives.

"I could hear my old lady screeching and hollering, 'Oh, my pie! my pie!' as she went reeling on down the mountain inside that pumpkin.

"Well, sir, there wasn't a thing I could do about it, so I figured there wasn't any use to get excited. I went to the ledge and looked after it a while as it went bumping and bounding down toward the valley, cutting a swath through the under-brush as it went.

"About halfway down I saw it bounce across the highway and crash into a covered wagon loaded with apples. Folks in the valley told me afterwards that apples rained down on 'em thick as hail for half an hour or so. They thought a miracle had happened up in the sky. Soon after that I lost sight of the thing, so I went on back to the barn.

"One look at my wagon told me I wasn't going to haul any pumpkins to the fair, but I didn't see any call to give up the trip. I could still go on muleback. The pumpkin had headed in that direction anyhow, and I thought I might as well jog down and see what had happened to my wife.

"Into the cabin I went and put on my store-bought Sunday clothes. As I was on my way out again, my eyes lit on a piecrust sitting there on the kitchen table. It was nice and brown and

crisp-looking and it came to me that this must have been what my wife was a-screeching about as she went rolling down the mountain. I picked it up, wrapped it carefully so it wouldn't break, and put it into my saddlebag.

"Then I straddled my mule and ambled on down the trail, wondering a mite as I jogged along where my old lady could have ended up.

"When I got down to Beaverdam I began to get a suspicion that she had rolled right onto the fairground. There was a hole in the side of the fence that would have accommodated an elephant, and the trail of wreckage inside the grounds looked like a hurricane had torn through. Folks were running around like excited ants trying to fix up the damage.

"I followed the trail of ruin and at the end of it, sure enough, there sat my wife amidst the wreckage of the pumpkin. It had smashed against a stone chimney.

" 'Oh my pie, my pie! Now I've got no pie to take to the fair,' she was still a-wailing.

" 'Why, honey, yes you have,' I said to her as I rode up. I put my hand into my saddlebag and brought out the pie-crust.

" 'But—but Hank,' she said. 'A pumpkin pie's got to have sugar and eggs and spices and I don't know what-all.'

" 'Not this pumpkin, honey,' I said to her. 'The pumpkins I raise are flavored already. You just scoop out one of these pieces and spread it in the crust "as is," and you'll have a finer, tastier pie than anybody at the fair.'

"Well, sir, she got up from there, brushed herself off a mite, straightened her hair a little, and fixed up that pie just as I told her to. You can see for yourself what the upshot was.

"Look over there now, across that table full of wild strawberry jam beside that fancy patchwork quilt hanging on the wall. There she stands. See that pie she's a-holding? That's the very pie and if it hasn't got a blue ribbon a-hanging to it I'll eat my Sunday pants."

"Well, Hank," said Mr. Zeke Calloway, sourly, "all I've got to say is, it's too bad they're not offering prizes for tall tales. If they were there'd be two blue ribbons in your family."

The Pudding That Broke Up the Preaching

Talk about puddings! There never was a more astonishing pudding than the one Ma Tolliver beat up for the all-day preaching that went on down in Possum Hollow Church on Thanksgiving Day. Folks came down to preachings from all over the countryside in those days, from Sandy Creek and Turkey Bottom and Huggins' Crossroads. They brought their dinners with 'em and between sermons and singing that went on morning and afternoon, they spread their victuals on the ground, picnic fashion, and had a real slapbang good dinner.

Everybody tried to outdo everybody else with their pies and cakes and roast turkey and what not, and Ma Tolliver laid off that Thanksgiving to have a pudding that would top everything else at the preaching. She started on it early Wednesday morning, mixing up her meal and molasses, cutting up peaches and nuts and such fixings to make it extra fancy. After she'd had it on the fire a spell, it came to her that she'd forgot to put the salt in it.

Now every good cook knows a pudding's not right without a pinch of salt, so Ma called out to her oldest girl. "Saphronie!"

she says, "I forgot the salt in the pudding and I'm out here picking a turkey with my fingers all stuck full of feathers. Run in the kitchen for me and put in a good big pinch of salt."

"Lawsy, Ma, I'm a-ironing my dress for the big doings tomorrow. If I stop now my iron'll get all cold." And she went on ironing as hard as she could.

"Hitty, you run in the kitchen and put some salt in the pudding for me," hollered Ma to the next oldest girl.

"I declare to goodness, Ma, I can't do it. I've just been to the witchwoman to get her to take the warts off my hands and she's smeared axle grease over both my hands and told me not to wash it off till I saw the evening star over my left shoulder. I can't pick up a pinch of salt with axle grease all over my hands."

By this time Ma was mighty nigh wore out with hollering but she decided to try once more. "You, Lucy! Can't you run in the kitchen and put some salt in the pudding for me?"

"Golly, Ma, I'm a-lying here in bed with cucumber peelings all over my face a-trying to bleach off the freckles before tomorrow. I can't get up now!"

"Sally!" Ma shouted to the youngest girl. "Hump yourself into the kitchen and throw some salt in the pudding for me."

"Goodness sakes, Ma, I'm a-working like fire to get my hair rolled up on old stockings, so's I'll have curls for the doings tomorrow. I ain't got time to salt the pudding!"

Since there weren't any more girls to ask, Ma hollered at her son, "Rufus, please go in the kitchen and throw a spoonful of salt into the pudding." But Rufus was busy, too.

He was a young fellow, just beginning to cotton to girls and do a little courting. "I swan, Ma," he called back, "I'm all full of bear's grease. Been slicking down my hair with it, and now I'm a-greasing my Sunday-go-to-meeting boots. I can't put any salt in any pudding now!"

By that time all the children were used up, and Ma began to holler at her old man. "Lem, can't you stop whatever you're doing and go put a spoonful of salt in the pudding?"

"Shucks, Ma, I'm a-cleaning my gun for tomorrow. S'posing a nice fat rabbit ran across the road whilst we're a-going. If my gun wasn't ready we'd miss a good rabbit stew for supper. Got my hands full of gun soot. I can't take care of your pudding now."

"Oh, tarnation!" Ma said to herself, clean out of patience. "I'll do it myself!" So she washed the feathers off her hands, and into the kitchen she marched. She got a good big pinch of salt, went over to the hearth where the pudding was boiling away in a pot swung over the fire, and threw it in.

Well, after a while Saphronie got her dress all done up, and she got to feeling a little ashamed that she hadn't done what Ma had asked her to. So she went over to the salt box, got a big pinch, and threw it into the pudding.

Hitty got to feeling bad about refusing Ma, too. "I reckon I could manage to get some salt in that pudding if I tried," she said. So she went into the kitchen, picked up a spoon with her black greasy hands, dipped up a good big dose of salt, and stirred it into the pudding.

Then Lucy, lying back on the bed with her face covered with cucumbers, got to thinking that she hadn't done right, not to help her ma when she was asked. So she got up, went to the hearth, and put some more salt in the pudding.

No sooner had she got out of the way, than Sally came into the kitchen with her hair done up in knobs all over her head. She got a good-sized pinch of salt and dropped it in the pudding.

Then Rufus got to thinking about it after he'd finished his boots. So into the kitchen he went and dipped up a good big tablespoonful. Being a man, he didn't know much about such things, and he thought you had to put as much salt in a pudding as in a pot of stew.

Pa's conscience got to hurting him, too, and as soon as his gun was all shined up and loaded, he clumped into the kitchen, dipped up a heaping spoonful of salt, and threw it over into the pudding.

At last the pudding was done. Ma took it off the fire. It turned out of the pot as pretty as you please.

"That's as fine a looking pudding as ever I saw!" Ma said. "With a pudding like that, I might even ask the preachers to have some tomorrow."

"Oh yes, do, Ma!" the girls exclaimed.

The next day was sparkling and sunny. Everybody set off, walking to the church. The preaching went fine. As soon as one preacher was winded, another one got up and took his place. By twelve o'clock they were all knocked out, so they called time out for Thanksgiving dinner.

Well, sir, Ma was so proud of that pudding that, sure enough, she invited all the preachers over to have some. There

were four of 'em, so she cut off four huge hunks and told 'em to dig in.

The first one that took a bite looked at Ma with his eyes popping half out of his head.

"You never tasted anything like it, now did you?" Ma asked proudly.

"No, sister, I never did, and that's a fact," the preacher said.

"Go on, don't be bashful, finish it up!" Ma urged and the poor fellow, not to hurt her feelings, took another bite and gulped it down.

Those four preachers sure proved their Christian feelings that day. All four of 'em choked down the pudding without saying a word against it.

After they'd staggered off toward the church, Ma cut some off for herself and passed each of her family a piece. Everybody took a bite and looked up, horrified. Then it came out how each of 'em had gone into the kitchen and salted the pudding.

Ma was mortified. "Too many cooks sure spoilt this pudding!" she said.

They spoilt the preaching, too, you can be sure of that. Those preachers didn't save any souls that afternoon. As soon as one of 'em would get himself worked up to a hollering pitch, he'd have to stop and whisper for a glass of water. There was so much water hauled up to the pulpit that day that folks stopped thinking about the preaching and began to wonder what the trouble was. Some took to counting the glasses.

What with preachers plagued with thirst and everybody whispering to each other asking questions, the meeting broke up 'way ahead of time. The tale about the pudding finally got around and ever since that time folks around Possum Hollow tell about Ma's pudding that broke up the big Thanksgiving all-day preaching.

The Bear and the Wildcat

"Things just happen to me," Hank Huggins said. "Peculiar happenstances swarm after me like flies after a barrel of molasses. Why, just buying a little piece of beefsteak once got me into the worst predicament you ever heard tell of!" Hank settled himself and began his tale.

"It happened when I was a-living over on the other side of Thunderhead Mountain. It was a far piece from there down to Asheville. In the fall of that year, after my apples were ripe, I loaded two bags full onto the old mule's back and rode on down to sell 'em.

"I got there all right and got a pocketful of cash money for my load. I bought me a few things I needed, salt and nails and whatnot. Then I said to myself, 'Now what can I buy to pleasure my old lady?' It came to me, of a sudden, that she hadn't had a taste of beefsteak in a coon's age. I went into a butcher's shop and had 'em cut me off a hunk. I put it in one of my saddlebags and off I set for home.

"Now it's a long pull up and over old Thunderhead. The road is rocky and sometimes there's no road at all—you have to splash along the creek bed. And it's wild and lonesome all the way. Well, sir, along toward dark, the mule began to act skeery and skittish-like.

" 'Some varmint's got wind of this piece of fresh meat!' I said to myself. 'Something's slipping through these bushes sure as shooting!'

"I hadn't more than got the words out of my mouth than up on a limb over the road I caught sight of a wildcat fixed for a spring. Now a wildcat's not very big—not much heftier than a house cat. But let me tell you, there's not a more ferocious critter in the entire length of the Blue Ridge country! With those hind claws of his, he can strip a man to ribbons in five minutes.

"Well, sir, the same minute I got sight of *him*, I heard a roar from the other side of the road. I looked that-a-way. Jumping Jehoshaphat, there was the biggest, blackest bear I ever laid eyes on!

"He made a spring for me, his mouth wide open. The wildcat sprang toward me from the other side. I ducked. The mule leaped. It was a clean miss! I was getting away from there lickety-split when I heard a great scratching and scrambling behind. I glanced back and I'll be blessed if that wildcat hadn't

leaped head-first right into the bear's open mouth. His head was stuck tight. There they were, a-rolling and a-tumbling. The bear was a-choking and the wildcat was a-stifling to death.

"The upshot of it was, I got home with the beefsteak, a wildcat, and a two-hundred-pound bear on my mule's back. My old lady made me a fur cap out of the cat skin. We got a fur robe big enough for a bedcover out of the bearhide. There was enough bear meat to feed a hundred and fifty people. So I broiled him over the coals and invited everybody within gunshot to come and help eat him up!"

A Tall Turnip

"All up and down the Blue Ridge Mountains the folks used to be scarified to poke their heads out-of-doors for fear of getting a stray bullet," said Hank Huggins. "That was when the Calloways and the Hugginses were a-doing some real feuding. Things have quieted down considerable since then. The two families have even come to speak to each other, and the young folks play ball and traipse around together somewhat. But there's some of the old feeling still left away down deep in every one of 'em. The Calloways are always trying to get ahead of the Hugginses in some way, and the Hugginses are just as set on outdistancing the Calloways, and usually they succeed —if I do say so as shouldn't, being a Huggins myself.

"When I looked out one day," Hank went on, "and saw old man Zeb Calloway a-planting turnips in a patch right next to my turnip patch, I suspected right away that he had a notion of outdoing me some way or other. And it turned out just as I'd figured it. He'd sent away to a mail-order house for some fancy turnip seed and he was allowing he'd raise some turnips that would make mine look like nubbins.

" 'That's a game two can play at,' I said to myself, and I straddled my gray mule and took a trip down to Asheville and bought myself a package of turnip seed just as fancy as his.

'And it's not all in the seed either!' I said. 'I aim to out-cultivate, out-fertilize, and out-water old man Calloway ten to one.'

"I soon found out this took harder work than I cared for, so I settled down to specialize on one turnip. I did all my work on that one turnip and, folks, you ought to have seen it grow! Within a month the part that stuck out of the ground was up to my knee—not counting the leaves that struck me around the shoulders. By midsummer it was up to my waist, and by early fall it was head-high. It was a world's wonder, and folks from all over the hill country came to see it. Old man Calloway was that put out he wouldn't even stick his head out the door.

"Come fall, that turnip was still a-growing. I reckon it kept on even after winter set in but after the first freeze I was distracted by something else and forgot all about it. I had a flock of twenty-seven sheep disappear right off the face of the earth and I spent every spare minute a-hunting for 'em. All winter long I hunted for those sheep, on the high crags, through the valleys, and in the deep coves; but nary a sign of 'em did I see. After a while I gave 'em up for lost.

"One day in late spring, old man Calloway dropped in, pretending to condole with me. 'Those sheep of yours have fallen off a cliff, like as not,' he said, shaking his head mournfully. 'Or else they've starved to death during this bitter cold weather. Now if you'd spent more time a-building a sheepfold and less time on that pithy overgrown turnip, you would have been better off.'

" 'Pithy!' I cried. 'That turnip's as sound as a dollar and you know it!'

" 'Nothing of the kind. It's pithy, and worm-eaten, too. I was a-looking at it only yesterday and I saw a wormhole big enough for a man to crawl into. And when I struck it with the flat of my hand, it sounded as hollow as a barrel. You should have known a monstrous overgrown thing like that wouldn't be fit to eat.'

"That fairly outraged me. 'I'll cut into that turnip right now,' I said, snatching up an ax and setting off for the turnip patch, 'and you can see for yourself whether it's hollow or not!' The old man followed along at my heels and my wife, hearing the argument, came running out the door and traipsed along, too.

"I had to admit when I got to the patch that the turnip did look a bit seedy. It was big, there was no gainsaying that— nigh as big as a house—but it had a thin, frail look about it like it was all gone inside and might cave in any moment. The wormhole was there just as Zeb had claimed, and I'm jiggered if we couldn't hear a crunching chewing sound as if there was a whole army of worms in there hard at work.

" 'Didn't I tell you so?' exclaimed the old man triumphantly. 'Pithy and full of worms—not fit for hogs to eat!'

"That made me really mad and I lifted my ax and split that turnip wide open.

"When it fell apart my wife let out a yell, 'Why, Hank, the sheep! There they are!'

"And sure enough, there they were, the whole flock of twenty-seven, all fat and sassy. There they'd been all winter long, sheltered from the cold, munching away, keeping plump and healthy on the insides of that turnip.

" 'Hollow and pithy, was it?' I said, turning to old man Calloway, 'How many turnips on your side of the fence would have kept a flock of sheep alive during a whole winter?'

"Well, sir, Zeb never said a word. He saw I had him and he just turned and shambled off towards home."

Saved by a Turkey

There never was a fellow like Jess Honeycutt for figuring himself out of a fix. Take the time he was left stranded in a rowboat in the middle of Dishpan Lake. He was all by himself with nary an oar for rowing, nor a pole to shove with. It was wintertime, too cold for swimming even if he'd known how, and there wasn't a cabin within hollering distance. There wasn't anything around but the wild and lonesome mountains. Now how was he to get out of such a predicament?

Many a man would have sat there in that boat till he starved to death or a search party came and rescued him. But not young Jess. No sir! He put on his thinking cap and before you could say Jack Robinson he was on his way home in a hurry —faster than if he hadn't lost his oars.

Here's how it all came about. You see, there was a turkey-shoot that day over at John Huggins' place t'other side of Dishpan Lake. Everybody else went the long way by the trail on yonder side of the mountain, but young Jess got into his little old pea-shell of a boat and rowed himself across the lake.

When he got there he found the young bucks from all the ridges and ranges around about, and everyone bent and determined to have that turkey. They had the bird tied down behind a log with only its head a-sticking up. Every man took

34

turn and turn about shooting at it, each one a-trying to hit the critter in the eye. But that old bird was a-trying just as hard not to be hit. He was the greatest dodger ever seen at a turkey-shoot.

As it so happened, the boys got to laughing and joking about that turkey a-dipping and a-dodging and a-outsmarting all their shooting.

"A critter as sharp as that hadn't ought to be shot at all," said young Jess.

All the other young fellows agreed. So they put up a paper bull's-eye and began to shoot at that instead. There was some mighty fancy shooting, I can tell you. But when it was all over, there was Jess Honeycutt's bullet spang in the middle of the bull's-eye. And for good measure, just to show it wasn't an accident, he stood off and shot his initials—J.H.—into the side of a great big pine tree. So they gave him the turkey,

feet tied together, but alive and kicking up a deuce of a fuss.

Golly, it was a big one, with a wingspread like an old baldy eagle. Young Jess was pleased a sight. "My wife's a-going to be tickled to death to have this bird," he said. He laid the critter down real careful in the bottom of the boat near the bow. Then he set to with his oars.

After he'd been out for around an hour and had got toward the center of the lake, that turkey got the notion he was tired of the whole idea. He didn't like boating, he didn't like having his feet tied together, and besides that it was getting along toward evening, the time when all fowl begin to think of climbing onto something high. And that bird was a-hankering to get outen the bottom of the boat. He began to flop and to flounder, and the first thing Jess knew he had scuffled up onto the prow of the boat. There he perched, wings spread out, ready to take off.

Jess dropped his oars. He jumped up, made a grab, and caught the turkey by the feet. He got him down into the bottom of the boat again and this time he trussed him up for sure and tied him down to a big stone he kept for anchoring the boat. Then he sat down again and looked around for his oars.

Not a sign of an oar did he see. He'd dropped 'em overboard when he jumped up to get the turkey and they'd floated clean away. He scanned the water every which way. Jess had never learned to swim and even if he'd known how, he'd have frozen to an icicle if he'd tried it in that icy water. So there he sat, with the mountains casting long shadows and the valleys filling up with darkness, and nary an idea how to get home.

"I could sit here on this lake until Judgment Day and not a soul would miss me," Jess said to himself. "If I don't get home tonight my wife will likely think I've decided to stay a few days hunting with John Huggins. And John will think I'm safe at home with my wife. Why, it might be two weeks or a month before folks begin to wonder where I am and get out a-looking for me."

With only the turkey and his gun out there in the middle of that lonely lake, and nary a thing to propel the boat, Jess knew he was in a fix for sure. But he was never one to give up when things looked tough. He was always one to say that where there was a will there was a way. So he sat down there and began to think up a way. And pretty soon, sure enough, he had an idea.

First he felt in his pocket to see if he had any rifle bullets. Yes, he did, two or three left from the turkey-shoot. Then he got up and examined the painter rope on the prow of his boat that he always used for tying up to the wharf. Yes, it was good and strong, strong enough to haul the boat through the water. He sighted toward shore to see if the boat was headed toward home, and it was. So then he rousted the turkey out of the bottom of the skiff and loosed him from the stone. After that he tied the critter's feet to the free end of the painter rope and set him onto the prow of the boat. Then he upped with his rifle and shot a blast into the air. On that quiet lake it boomed out with a noise fit to wake the dead. It scared that old turkey outen five years' growth. He leaped into the air, spread his wings, and took off. It was nighttime and he was a-hankering to get home to his roosting place. I reckon he never had no idea which-a-way it was, but he knew good and well it wasn't out there in the middle of Dishpan Lake.

Jess just sat back in that little boat while the turkey made for the land. He never had an easier nor a smoother ride. When he felt the boat bump ashore, he got out and hauled in the turkey on the end of the painter. He tucked it under his arm and traipsed along home.

Just as he expected, Jess' wife was pleased a sight to get

the turkey. Right away she began to plan how she'd cook him for dinner and have a big to-do. But Jess didn't have any heart for eating that bird. He said no, he'd rather keep him for a pet. And that's what he did. When at last the fowl died of old age, Jess buried him under a catalpa tree and put up a stone that read:

"True and faithful feathered friend
He saved me from an awful end."

The Blizzard of '98

Hank Huggins sat on the porch of his cabin one cold March day, with his feet propped on the rail. He was looking out over the long ranges of the Blue Ridge Mountains.

"Cold enough for you, Hank?" asked a neighbor who had stopped to borrow a pint of lamp oil.

"Why, no," said Hank. "My mind was just working back to the blizzard of '98. Folks that didn't see that blizzard haven't got any idea of what cold weather is." Hank settled himself for the following tale.

"It came on suddenly. One minute, it was near about as warm as summer. The next, everything was frozen stiff and hanging with icicles a foot long. Some cattle that were a-pasturing out on a hillside right near my cabin piled up on top of one another to get warm. They froze into a pyramid as hard as a rock. But the freakiest thing I ever heard of was what happened to my old lady.

"I was across the valley, where you see that cabin with the smoke a-rising from the chimney. A-walking, it's a mighty far piece over there. But as the crow flies, it's near, within hollering distance. Well, sir, when my wife saw the sky darkening all of a sudden and heard the wind whistling down from the high peaks, it scarified her half outen her wits. She ran into the front yard and yelled across the valley for me to come home.

"I was a-standing in the front yard across the way. I saw her come into our yard. I saw her jaws a-working like she was talking. But I never heard a sound. Anyway, one look at the weather told me I'd never get home before the storm broke. I hustled into the house with my neighbor and we slammed the door. Well, sir, just as I told you, it was a blizzard to end all blizzards.

"After the worst was over, the sun came out. I set off for home. Everything was coated with ice and a-glittering like crystal. I slid downwards through a glass forest and chipped my way up the other side. Everything you looked at was like an ornament to put on the mantelpiece.

"When I got home, the old lady was in a temper. 'Why didn't you answer when I called you?' she shouted at me as

I came in the door. 'Seems you could have said yes or no or something!'

" 'I didn't hear you say anything,' I threw back at her.

" 'Don't tell me you didn't hear anything!' she cried. 'I've been hollering across that valley too many years to think I couldn't make myself heard!'

"Well, we talked it back and forth, she claiming that she hollered for me, I allowing that she never made a sound. We were still at it hot and heavy when a queer noise in the air made us stop stock-still. At first it sounded like an old phonograph record starting off slow-like. Then it picked up. And out there in the blue air, between the two mountains, came a shout, 'Hank! You, Hank Huggi-i-ns! Look at the sky! It's a-going to snow! You come on right now before you get caught away from home!'

"It was my old lady's voice—to the life. And she hadn't said a word! We looked at each other, our eyes fairly popping. 'They're my very words!' she whispered as though she'd heard a ghost. 'They're the very words I hollered when the blizzard was a-blowing down!'

"Well, sir, for a minute there, my brains were fairly scattered. I didn't know what to think. Then it came to me.

" 'Why, of course,' I said. 'Can't you see what happened? That blizzard was so cold and it came up so suddenly that it froze your words in mid-air. They never got to the other side. Now, with the weather warming up, they've thawed out.' "

"Well, Hank," said the neighbor, picking up his bottle of lamp oil, and setting off down the path, "I agree with you. The folks that missed that blizzard don't know what cold weather really is!"

Old Plott

For as long as he could remember, young Jess Honeycutt had been hearing about the train. It passed through the city forty miles on yonder side of the mountain. Everybody that came back from there had something to tell about it.

"She's a sight to behold," they said. "She's got one eye right in the middle of her forehead. Go to see her in the nighttime. There she comes, down the track, glaring like a one-eyed wildcat staring into a pine torch. And racket. Whee! She comes a-raring like a square dance on a tin roof!"

Jess sure did have a hankering to see that train-critter, and one time when his wife went off to visit her folks he allowed it was his chance and he was a-going. He stuck the frying pan up the chimney, hid the ax in a crotch of the tree, whistled up old Plott, his bear dog, and off he put. As he trudged on down the trail Jess got to thinking that it might not be a good idea to take his dog along. How could he prepare old Plott's mind for the sight of the train? The thing might scarify him to the point of addling his wits. He might run clean away and never come back. Jess didn't want anything like that to happen. Old Plott was the best bear dog anywhere in the Blue Ridge Mountains. Everybody knew it, and Jess loved him like a brother.

By this time, Jess had got down the mountain as far as the cabin where old man Gruber lived. The idea came to him that he might ask the old man to keep Plott until he got back from his travels. Yes, that's what he'd do. No use taking chances with such a valuable dog.

He opened the front gate, walked up to Mr. Gruber's cabin and knocked at the door. It opened a crack and a gun barrel came poking through.

Young Jess gave a start. He backed away. "Hold on there, Mr. Gruber, hold on a minute. I don't mean you no harm."

"Who is it then?" came old man Gruber's voice from inside and it sounded mighty mean.

"It's me, Jess Honeycutt."

"Oh, so it's you, young Jess!" Old man Gruber stuck his head out the door. "Where are your raisings, young feller? That ain't no way to act, to come a-knocking at the door without even a whoop or a holler. How's a man to know if it's friend or foe? Mind your manners next time and give a holler before you open the gate."

"Yes, sir, Mr. Gruber, I sure will. I beg your pardon for giving you a scare."

"All right then, young Jess, all right. Now what is it you've come for?"

"I'm off for a trip, Mr. Gruber and I just wondered if you'd do me a favor while I'm away in foreign parts?"

"A favor? I don't know about that." Old man Gruber drew in his head and began to shut the door.

"I'll pay you well if you'll help me out, Mr. Gruber!" cried young Jess.

"Oh, that's different now." Mr. Gruber looked out again. "What is it you want me to do? What's the favor?"

"I was going to ask you to keep old Plott for me while I'm away."

"Old Plott? You want me to keep old Plott whilst you're away?" A greedy gleam came into old man Gruber's eyes. "Bring him right in, Jess. That's a favor I won't charge you for. I'll keep him here and treat him as kindly as if he were my own child. I sure will."

"That's mighty nice of you, Mr. Gruber." Jess was real pleased. He whistled old Plott into the cabin and shut the door on him. Then he went along on his journey, satisfied and easy in his mind. He clean forgot what folks said about old man Gruber, that he would steal the pennies outen a blind beggar's hat; that he was the meanest, stingiest, cheatin'est old man in seven counties.

A few days later, down the trail again came young Jess. He was footsore and dusty. He'd been over the mountain to the city. He'd seen the train and he'd had enough of traveling. He stopped at old man Gruber's gate and gave a whoop and a holler.

Old man Gruber stuck his head out the door.

"Heigh-oh there, Mr. Gruber. Well, I'm back from my trip." He opened the gate and walked up the path.

"Howdy, young Jess, howdy. I reckon you've seen a sight, I reckon you have. Well, come around and tell me all about it one of these days." Old man Gruber drew in his head and began to shut the door.

"Hold on there, Mr. Gruber, hold on!" Young Jess stuck his foot in the crack. "What about my dog Plott? Where's old Plott? I've come for him."

"Old Plott, old Plott?" Mr. Gruber scratched his head and pretended to think. "Oh, yes, I declare I near 'bout forgot old Plott. Son, I sure am sorry to have to tell you about old Plott."

"What's the matter? What's happened? He ain't run away, has he?"

"Worse than that, son—"

"He ain't been hurt now, has he?"

Old man Gruber didn't say anything. He just looked down at the ground and shook his head in a mournful way.

"You ain't trying to tell me old Plott is dead now, are you, Mr. Gruber?" cried young Jess.

"I'm sorry to have to tell you, son, but he sure is. Dead as a doornail."

Tears came to young Jess' eyes. He felt as though a mule had kicked him right in the middle of his stomach. "Don't tell me, Mr. Gruber. That dog was everything to me. I wouldn't have taken a pretty for him."

"Well, son, it's the truth. He's dead."

"How did it happen, Mr. Gruber?"

"Why, son, the day you left I shut old Plott up in a little old house here on the place. I'd been renting it to some powerful dirty folks and they'd left it chockablock full of bedbugs. Those bugs hadn't had nothing to eat for the longest time. I reckon they were mortal hungry. Anyway, they set onto old Plott in the night and ate him up, hair, hide, and all. Wasn't anything left but his bones."

Jess turned about to go home. "Those bugs don't know what they've done to me!" He stumbled down the path with hanging head. He glanced back as he opened the gate. Mr. Gruber was grinning from ear to ear, as though he had done something mighty smart and was real pleased with himself.

That set young Jess to studying. He stood a minute with his hand on the gate, then he turned around and walked up the path again.

"Mr. Gruber, I declare to goodness, this has hit me mighty hard. And I'm clean wore out with traveling. I feel so bad I don't know as I can get home. You know it's a mighty steep climb from here up to my cabin there on the mountain.

Wouldn't you lend me your mule to ride on the rest of the way?"

"I don't know about that, now, young Jess. I need my mule here to home. Got to do some plowing today. Got to plow every day this week."

Young Jess stepped up on the porch. "Well then, Mr. Gruber, I reckon you'll just have to give me some dinner and some supper later on and put me up for the night. I haven't got the strength to go a step farther."

"Now, now, young Jess, you ain't that bad off." Mr. Gruber looked worried.

"I sure am, Mr. Gruber, I'm laid low. I'll have to stay the night with you, I sure will."

"No, young Jess, you can't do that. No, you can't. Maybe I'd better lend you my mule after all. Will you bring him back tomorrow sure and certain?"

"Sure as shootin', Mr. Gruber. Why would you ask such a thing? You know I'm as honest as the day is long, just like Pap and my old grandpap before me."

Old man Gruber led out his mule. Young Jess straddled him and off he went, plodding up the trail toward home.

On the following day, old man Gruber got up bright and early. He looked up the trail to see if young Jess was on the way with his mule. Not a sign of him did he see.

"Now, that's no way to do—to keep my mule till half the day is gone! Maybe he won't get here till afternoon," he grumbled to himself and he found some work to do around the house.

When nighttime came and still no Jess and no mule, old man Gruber fussed and fumed. "That young scamp, a-keeping my mule right now during planting time. What's he up to, I'd like to know?"

The next day he leaped up as soon as the sun peeped over

the ridge and ran out to see if young Jess was on the way. No, he wasn't. And the next day he didn't come either. Old man Gruber was mad a sight. "That cheating young rascal, I'll have the law on him, that I will. He'll pay me hard money for every day he keeps my mule!"

Well, day by day went by with never a sign of Jess and the mule. With his creaky joints, old man Gruber knew well enough he'd never make it up the steep trail to the cabin where Jess lived, and every day that passed he got madder and madder.

Then one morning, after the sun was well up in the sky, he looked out the window and there was young Jess sauntering along the road as though he didn't have a care in the world nor a thought for Mr. Gruber's mule.

Old man Gruber ran out of the house without even stopping to put his shoes on. "Oh there you are, you young scallawag! Where's my mule, now, where is he, I'd like to know?"

Young Jess stopped in the middle of the road. He looked at Mr. Gruber in a surprised sort of way. Then he scratched his head and pretended to think. "Your mule, Mr. Gruber? Oh, yes, I declare I near 'bout forgot your mule. I sure am sorry to have to tell you about him, Mr. Gruber."

"What do you mean? What's happened to my mule?"

Young Jess didn't answer. He just looked down at the ground and shook his head in a mournful way.

"You haven't lost my mule in the mountains? You haven't let him fall off a cliff, have you?" shouted old man Gruber.

"Worse than that, Mr. Gruber. Worse than that," Jess said sadly.

"You ain't trying to tell me my mule is dead now, are you?" screamed the old man.

"I've got a mighty strong suspicion he is—dead as a doornail. But I don't know for sure, Mr. Gruber. No, I don't. A mighty curious thing happened to your mule. It sure did."

"I don't believe it! I don't believe nary a word you say, Jess Honeycutt. You've stole my mule and I'll have you jailed!" screeched old man Gruber. "Come on now, come right on. I'm going to haul you down the road to Squire Meekins' house. He'll fix you for stealing my mule." He grabbed young Jess by the arm and began to drag him down the road.

When they got to the crossroads where Squire Meekins lived, old man Gruber stood at his gate and hollered, "Squire Meekins! Come out, come out here right now. I want you to 'tend to this mule-thief!" And there he stood a-shouting and a-vaporing until Squire Meekins came out on the porch to see what all the racket was about.

"I want you to throw young Jess in the jailhouse, Squire!" Old man Gruber shook his fist in the air and stomped his bare feet. "I want you to haul him off to jail right now!"

"Now, now, Mr. Gruber—" began Squire Meekins in a kindly voice.

"He stole my mule!" shrieked old man Gruber. "He borrowed my mule and won't bring him back. He says something curious happened to him. 'T ain't so. He's stole him. He's a plain mule-thief and I want the law on him!"

Squire Meekins held up his hand. "Calm yourself, Mr. Gruber, calm yourself. Let's get at both sides of this dispute. What's this all about, young Jess, what's happened to Mr. Gruber's mule? You tell me now, straight out."

"Well, it happened like this, Squire Meekins. As I was a-riding along home the other day after Mr. Gruber lent me that mule, I saw some turkey buzzards sort of sailing around up there in the sky. They kept circling lower and lower. I never thought nothing about it until they were right over my head. It came to me then that it was mighty peculiar how close they'd come. I could have reached up and grabbed one. All of a sudden one of 'em swooped down. He grabbed Mr. Gruber's mule by the tail. He upended that mule and heaved me off, right over the critter's head. Then he went sailing off with that mule, a-flying fast and a-crowing like a rooster!"

"Hold on there, young Jess," exclaimed Squire Meekins. "I've seen many a turkey buzzard in my life, but nary one that could crow like a rooster!"

"As I'm a-living, that buzzard went a-flying off with that mule," young Jess insisted. "And with all the other buzzards following after. Last I saw of 'em they were a-clearing the top of Old Baldy Mountain. I reckon those buzzards hadn't had anything to eat in the longest time and they was mortal hungry. By this time you can be sure they've eaten Mr. Gruber's mule and picked his bones."

"You hear that, Squire Meekins?" yelled old man Gruber. "He expects us to believe a gally-whopper like that. He stands there and tells such buncombe with a straight face!"

"If a bunch of hungry bedbugs can eat up a full-grown dog like what happened to my old Plott, then a bunch of hungry

buzzards can fly off with a mule and pick his bones," said young Jess.

It all came out then, how old man Gruber had acted about old Plott.

"What's sauce for the goose is sauce for the gander," said young Jess. "If my dog comes back after being eat by bedbugs, then maybe the mule will come back after being eat by the buzzards."

And that's just how it turned out. Squire Meekins made old man Gruber fetch Plott from the woods where he'd hid him and then young Jess brought back the mule. Maybe you think old man Gruber learned a lesson from all this. But no, folks in the mountains say he's still as mean and stingy and cheating as ever.

The Popcorn Patch

"I had an old mule once upon a time that fooled himself clean to death," said Hank Huggins. "It happened down in Cade's Cove where I had planted me a little patch of corn, the kind that's used for popping. It was a hot day. I didn't want to go out plowing that morning, but my old lady got after me.

" 'Hank,' she said, 'If you don't get out and plow that field of popcorn, the weeds will take it and the young'uns won't have any corn to pop at Christmas time.'

"I wasn't in the notion, I can tell you that. I saw the day was going to be a scorcher. But once my old lady has set her mind to something, there's no peace until it's done. So I went out, hitched up the mule, and set off to plow the cornfield.

"Heavens to Betsy, it was hot in that cove! The mountains standing up all around kept out every breath of breeze. The place held the heat like an oven. July flies were a-droning in the trees and the leaves hung as limp as a dog's tongue. It would be hard to say which was hotter, me or that old mule. Up and down the rows we went, a-toiling and a-sweating.

"Along towards noon it was broiling for certain. Even the old logs and stumps began to crawl off in the shade. Suddenly I heard a crackling sound in the air. Before I could figure out what had happened, white flakes were a-flying all around.

At first, I thought it was a snowstorm. Then I realized what it was: The blazing sun had set that corn a-popping, and it was falling like a snowstorm.

"That old mule of mine, he stopped and looked around. Then he began to shiver. He thought for sure he'd been overtaken by a howling blizzard. He stood there and squinched himself all up, like critters do when it's real cold.

" 'Get along there!' I hollered at him. 'It's nothing but popcorn!'

"But the poor thing couldn't understand. He'd never seen any popcorn before and he thought it was snow. He just stood there, shaking and shivering in every limb. I couldn't do a thing with him. It was a crying shame. Before I could get that critter unhooked from the plow and out of there, he gave right up. He lay down in the row and froze to death—all covered up with popcorn."

The Bear in the Black Hat

Seems like folks were always a-picking on Slocum Jones. It wasn't that he was small and helpless—far from it! He was a big, hulking fellow who shambled around like a bear. But his size didn't help him any. His wife, Addie, found fault with everything he did.

If he brought home coffee from the store, she said she had plenty in the house getting stale. If he got molasses, she quarreled with him for wasting money. If he had a grain of git-up-and-git, she told him, he could go out in the woods and find a wild beehive. If he put on his old black slouch hat and went out to the fields to work, she shouted at him a dozen things he should be doing around the house. If he worked around the house, she told him they were likely to be put off the land next year because he didn't get out and work the field. Nothing he did was right.

His landlord, old man Jackson, treated him no better than his wife. If Slocum planted corn, old man Jackson came stumping with his gold-headed cane and told him he was a-wearing out the land planting the same thing every year. If he planted peanuts or cotton, the old man came complaining that he was a blockhead to put peanuts and cotton in when the price was so low. He said he didn't know why he kept renting his land to such a dunderhead.

The only place Slocum could take refuge from all the quarreling and complaining and faultfinding was out in the woods. When it got to the point where he thought he couldn't stand it another minute, he'd wait until Addie wasn't looking then he'd take his gun down from the rack over the mantel, pull his hat over his eyes, motion silently to old Blue, his hunting dog, and take to the mountains. There they'd stay all day long and sometimes two days at a time. Then they'd come creeping humbly back home. Sometimes Slocum would have a rabbit to offer Addie on his return, or a string of squirrels to make a stew for old man Jackson. He always hoped they'd be thankful for the treat and maybe excuse him for his absence. But it never happened that way. Addie screamed at him that he would leave them all to starve to death with his worthless behavior. And old man Jackson threatened him with his gold-headed cane and told him he needed a good thrashing. And so it went with Slocum Jones until life was not worth living and it got so he was out in the woods half the time.

Then came a day that changed everything.

Slocum was hunting not far from home when he caught sight of a bear moseying along through the huckleberry bushes. His heart gave a bump. "It would sure put me in right with Addie if I could get that bear!" he thought. "There's nothing she likes better than some nice tender bear steaks. And a good warm bearskin to cover the bed of a winter's night would be a real handsome present!" He watched until the bear stood still to examine a hollow tree. Then he lifted his gun and drew a careful bead.

"Snap!" The gun didn't fire.

'Oh, tarnation! I've run out of shells!" Slocum was mighty put out.

Now what to do? He didn't mean to lose that bear if he could help it. Motioning old Blue to keep quiet, he crept along after the critter, watching where it went.

After meandering around for a spell, the bear clawed his way up an old tree broken off at the top and let himself down inside it.

Now Slocum hadn't been wandering the woods for nothing. He understood right away that there was a wild beehive in the tree. The bear was after honey. And right away Slocum got an idea. If he could stop up the top of the tree with something or other, maybe he could trap the bear. It might keep him there until he could get home and bring some ammunition.

Slocum hurried cautiously to the foot of the tree. Inside he could hear the bear greedily guzzling honey. He quickly chose a jagged rock, buttoned it into his coat, slung the coat over his back, and tied the sleeves around his neck. Then silently he shinned up the tree. He jammed the rock into the hole at the top. It fitted all right except for one place. At one side, a hole was left about the size of a man's head.

Inside the tree the bear stopped eating. He began to rustle around uneasily.

That critter's got suspicious in there. He may pop out, mad as a hornet, right into my face, thought Slocum.

There was no time to bring another stone to cover the hole. Without a second thought, Slocum snatched off his hat. There happened to be a jagged edge of the rock sticking up on one side of the hole, and a jagged piece of the tree on the other. Slocum fitted his hat over the two jutting pieces and jerked it down. It fitted as neatly as a glove and stuck tight. The hole was covered. Then he shinned down from the tree in a hurry and took off for home.

Just before he got there, he began to think about his hat. What would Addie say if he arrived without it? She'd never in the world believe he'd used it to trap a bear.

"She'll say I've lost it. She'll say I ought to be ashamed of myself to lose a good hat. She'll kick up a deuce of a racket." Slocum went slower and slower as he got nearer home. The thought of facing Addie without his hat made him so miserable that he finally decided not to go home at all. It was getting along toward sundown. He lay down with old Blue in a pile of leaves and slept there all night.

Meanwhile the bear was making a mighty effort to get out of the hollow tree. He humped himself against the stone but it wouldn't move. Then he put his head against the hat and shoved. Yes, it gave a little. The top of his head came through into Slocum's hat. He strained mightily with his shoulders and the stone flew out. He was free. But the hat was stuck on the top of his head. It frightened him at first and he ran through the bushes as fast as he could go, hoping it would fall off. But it stayed on his head and after a while he got used to it and understood that it would do him no harm. He began to feel hungry after all his struggles to get out, and his running through the scrub, and started out in search of something to eat. He wandered on and on, but could not find even so much as a blackberry. At last he found himself on the edge of a little farm. By chance, it happened to be the place where Slocum lived.

It was getting dusk as the bear rambled into the back yard. He sniffed. There was a nice smell of honey on the air. Inside the kitchen Addie was setting out an earthenware jar of honey for her supper. The bear sniffed and sniffed again. He traced the smell to the kitchen door and peered inside. No one was there. Addie had gone into the bedroom to light a lamp. On the table, set out invitingly, was the pot of honey. The bear ambled into the room and stuck his paw into the pot.

In the next room, Addie heard a noise. She left off lighting the lamp and poked her head into the half-dark kitchen. The first thing she spied was her husband's black hat and a dark form bending over the honeypot.

"Oh, so here you are, you worthless man," cried Addie. "Staying out all day in the woods and now stealing my honey like an ordinary thief!" She rushed into the kitchen, grabbed the honeypot out of the bear's paws, and fetched him a hard slap in the face.

"Gr-r-r-r!" The bear caught poor Addie around the waist. He gave her such a hug that her ribs cracked. Then he threw her into the corner against the wall, seized the honeypot, and shuffled out the door. Poor Addie was flabbergasted. She'd

never in her life expected Slocum to behave in that way. She was scared and pleased at the same time. Who would have thought he had it in him to give her such a hug and then throw her down like a sack of meal? She looked out the door but the bear was gone.

Night fell, but the moon was out and all was bright and silvery. The bear ambled on. He was still hungry. The honey left in Addie's pot had not nearly filled him up. He passed along near old man Jackson's pigpens. The sound of the pigs grunting sleepily gave him an idea. A nice fat shoat would make a wonderful supper. He shuffled over to the pen, climbed the rail fence, and grabbed the fattest one.

What a squealing those hogs put up! The bear was just climbing out of the pen when old man Jackson came on the run.

"Oh, so it's you!" In the moonlight he caught sight of a dark form wearing Slocum's black hat. "So now you've taken to stealing. You'll carry off my pig, will you!" The old man gave the bear a crack over the skull with his gold-headed cane.

"Gr-r-r-r!" The bear let out a roar. He dropped the pig and went for old man Jackson. He made a great swipe with his claws. It tore the old man's vest and his shirt wide open and scratched a streak down the middle of his stomach. Then the bear lifted the unlucky landlord and threw him into the muddy wallow with the pigs. Then, feeling a little upset with the crack on the head, he took out for the woods.

"Oh, lawsy," groaned old man Jackson. "The worm has turned." He picked himself out of the mud, climbed out of the pigpen, and tottered back to the house.

All this time, poor Slocum had been lying fast asleep in the leaves. When he woke up on the following morning, what should he see lying nearby but his old black hat. The bear had scraped it off on a low-hanging limb as he ran through the bushes on his way to the hills. Slocum was overjoyed. He picked up the hat and put it on. It gave him the courage to go home.

As he went shuffling along, he hoped that Addie wouldn't be at the house when he got there. If she were down at the springhouse getting the butter, or in the garden picking turnip greens, he could steal in, get his gun shells, and get away without being seen. But no, there she was, standing in the kitchen.

To his surprise, she was all prettied up and smiling the way she had not done since they were married. She had on her Sunday-go-to-meeting dress and her hair was all crimped and curled.

"I'm so glad to see you, honey—er, darling," she corrected herself, remembering how she'd snatched the honeypot. She took him by the arm, and led him into the kitchen. "Do sit down, you must be hungry after being away so long." She set out a plate of stewed chicken with dumplings that she'd already fixed for him.

Slocum was astonished. He wondered if he was on the earth or if he had died and gone to heaven.

After a wonderful meal it came to him that he hadn't fed old man Jackson's pigs for two days hand running. He hurried out of the house, got some corn and went to the pigpen.

"Oh, there you are!" Jackson came stumping along with his gold-headed cane, all smiles. "Right on the job as usual. I never saw such a man for work." Oh, he was full of kind speeches, was old man Jackson.

What had happened to everybody overnight? Slocum Jones was too amazed for words, but he thought it best not to spoil his luck by asking questions. From then on, there were only kind words and compliments for Slocum Jones. Addie made it so pleasant for him around home that he scarcely ever took to the woods. Old Blue got fat and lazy from lying around. But Slocum got so he went working in the fields everyday. His crops began to turn out the best of any for miles around. The upshot of it was that he and Addie and old man Jackson became so prosperous they had fried ham and gravy for breakfast, even on weekdays, and chicken and dumplings for dinner.

The Short Horse

Uncle Bridger was getting ready to go to a corn-shucking party at Turkey Creek. His bony nag was hitched to the spring wagon, and his wife and children and many of his relatives were seated in it on the heaped-up hay. Uncle Bridger shouted to the nag, and they were off at a trot.

A little way down the road, they met a good friend.

"Hey, Jess!" Uncle Bridger hauled back on the reins. The nag halted. "Come on and go with us to the corn-shucking."

"Gosh, Uncle Bridger," said Jess regretfully, "I just hired a horse from old man Gruber to ride to the shucking. But I'd a heap rather go with you all." He looked at the merry wagon-load with a long face.

"Go and tell old man Gruber you've changed your mind about hiring the horse," urged Uncle Bridger. "We'll wait for you."

"I've already paid him the money. That old man is as tight as the bark on a tree; he'd never give it back to me." Jess shook his head with a worried frown.

"Oh, I reckon you could talk him out of it," said Uncle Bridger.

"That old skinflint? Not a chance."

"Come on, I'll go with you. We'll see what we can do. There are more ways than one of skinning a bear."

Uncle Bridger threw the reins to his wife and climbed over the wagon wheel. He and Jess walked back a piece to the log cabin surrounded by a cornfield. They stood at the gate and gave a whoop and a holler: "Mr. Gruber, oh say, Mr. Gruber!"

Old man Gruber opened the cabin door and came shuffling out.

"Howdy, Mr. Gruber. How are you?" Uncle Bridger greeted him.

"Ain't real pert, but making out somehow."

"That's good, Mr. Gruber. We can't expect too much in this world. Well, Mr. Gruber, Jess and I came to take a look at that horse he's hired to ride to the corn-shucking."

"Don't see why you've got to look at him; he's hired and paid for," grumbled old man Gruber. But he led them out to the stable and showed them the horse.

Uncle Bridger carefully examined the horse. Then with both hands spread out as a measure, he spaced him from head to tail. "This horse won't do. He's too short," he announced at last.

"What do you mean— 'he's too short?'" asked old man Gruber. "He's just like any other horse."

"No, he's a mite shorter," declared Uncle Bridger. He measured off the horse again. "Now, this place is for Jess, here. Here's space for me. His wife could sit here. There ain't much room left for my wife, and she don't aim to be left at home. Then where's Grandpap going to sit? He wants to go, too."

"What-what's this?" sputtered old man Gruber. "You aim to mount five people on my horse?"

"Only five," replied Uncle Bridger, "that is, unless Granny decides to go. But she's had a misery in her back the last two days so it could be she wouldn't go. So I reckon it'll be five."

"Oh no, you don't! No five people are a-going to ride any horse of mine!"

"Why, Mr. Gruber, that ain't many. I've rode six on a horse many a time. You can't back out now, Mr. Gruber, the horse is paid for!" exclaimed Uncle Bridger.

"Oh yes, I can." Mr. Gruber stuck his hand into his pocket and brought out some bills. "Here's your money back."

"But, Mr. Gruber, how'll we get to the shucking?" cried Uncle Bridger.

"Go hire yourself an elephant. That's the only critter I know of could carry a crowd like that."

And old man Gruber thrust the money into Jess' hands.

How Pa Learned to Grow
Hot Peppers

Pa Puckett had already gone out to work in the cornfield, but Ma and the young'uns, Mary and John and Alfred and Luli, were still at the breakfast table. They were trying to eat their sausages, but not doing very well at it. Mostly they were just pushing them around their plates because the sausages didn't have any flavor. The pepper in them was flat and tasteless and that made the sausages flat and tasteless.

"I declare," said Ma, "it's a mystery to me why your pa can't grow good hot peppers. The Calloways have good peppers, and the Honeycutts and the Grubers. Seems like everybody in the mountains can grow real good hot peppers except your pa. I just don't understand it."

"Maybe the ground ain't right," said Mary, who was fourteen years old.

" 'T ain't that," Ma said. 'He's planted 'em here and there, a different part of the farm every year and they always turn out the same; poor weak plants with only a few puny little peppers, as tasteless as sawdust."

"Does he plow good and deep?" asked John, who was twelve.

"Does he put on plenty of fertilizer?" said Alfred, who was eight.

"Does he plant the seed early in the morning while the ground is wet?" chirped Luli, who was six.

"He does everything just right," Ma told them. "He does everything just like other folks. But *their* fields will have big, red, healthy peppers, full of sting, and Pa's will be just the same as ever."

Mary shook her head sadly. John and Alf and Luli looked downhearted.

It was too bad about Pa's peppers. Folks in the backwoods needed good hot peppers. Every cabin had two or three strings of 'em hanging in the kitchen beside the bunches of dried string beans, called leather britches, and the garlands of onions with their tails plaited tight together. Red pepper sprinkled on the meat after it was killed in the wintertime helped to preserve it. And what good was a pot of turnip greens and fat bacon in the spring without a douse of good hot pepper vinegar? That pepper vinegar cut the grease and made the dinner set well on the stomach. And sausages? Without red pepper, a sausage wasn't a sausage at all.

Ma and the young'uns looked down at their sausages. They just weren't fitten to eat.

"It's enough to make a preacher kick," said little Luli.

"Luli!" Ma was shocked at such a saying.

"I reckon it *does* make Pa kick," Alfred said.

"No, it doesn't," Ma replied. "Nothing ever riles your pa. He's the mildest man ever I saw. If Mr. Gruber had a pepper crop turn out the way ours does, he'd be yelling and kicking up a dust about it. Mr. Calloway, too, and Mr. Honeycutt. They'd be stomping around something terrible. But not your pa. He's never lost his temper in his life."

"And now he's going to plant peppers tomorrow?" Mary asked. "Ain't that what he said?"

"That's what he said," Ma replied. "I just wish I knew what to do to break his bad luck."

"Listen, Ma," Mary leaned forward and whispered across the table. "Why don't we go to see the granny-witch? Why don't we go over to Bat Cave and ask the granny-witch how come Pa can't seem to grow good peppers?"

"Oh, my!" Ma looked shocked.

"Let's do, Ma, let's do!" cried John and Alf and Luli.

"It's a far piece over to Bat Cave," objected Ma.

"We can make it," cried the young'uns. "Let's get off right now."

"Lawsy me!" moaned Ma. "I haven't ever been to a granny-witch, never in my whole life."

"Come on, Ma, lets go before the sun gets high."

"Well—" Ma looked thoughtful. "I've tried everything else. I reckon it wouldn't do any harm."

The children jumped up with a yell. "We're a-going, we're a-going!"

"We'll have to fix up a snack to eat along the way. You get at it, young'uns, while I tidy the house." Ma got up and began to bustle around, washing the dishes and setting the cabin to rights.

The children sliced some ham and put it between biscuits. They wrapped them in cornhusks and packed them in a basket. Then they were ready to go.

"You reckon I ought to tell Pa we're a-going?" Ma hesitated.

"No, no, let's just go along!" The young'uns were afraid Pa would call off the whole expedition.

"Well then, I'll just leave his dinner ready for him on the

table." Ma set out a ham bone, some turnip greens, and a pone of corn meal.

"I'll have to carry the granny-witch a present," Ma said. "If you want a granny-witch to help you out, you'd better have a present for her. Now what'll we take?" She looked at the children thoughtfully.

"A mess of collard greens from the garden," said Mary.

"And a rutabaga," John added.

"That's just the thing!" Ma went out to the garden, pulled up the rutabaga, a nice big yellow one, and cut the heads of collard greens.

It was a fine day and off they set, footing it over the mountains. The children went zigzagging up the steep sides and scampering along the ridges with Ma puffing on behind. Then they went, trembly-kneed, down the other side. Along creeks and brooks they waded, splashing and scaring the minnows, and along toward midday they came to the dark cave where the granny-witch lived.

They all huddled fearful-like in front of the cave.

"I declare, young'uns," Ma said, "maybe we ought to go on back home and not bother this old granny-witch. She may not like having folks bother her."

"Shucks, Ma, go on and call her."

"She's just an old woman. Maybe she's lonesome for company," said Mary.

"I don't see any vegetable garden around here," said Alf. "Maybe she's a-hankering for some collard greens."

"And some rutabaga, too!" chirped Luli.

"Maybe she is, young'uns." Ma began to feel braver. She looked toward the cave and squeaked out, "Granny, oh, Granny!"

"Aye?" replied a cracked old voice in the cave.

Ma's eyes got big but she called again, "Come out, Granny, we've got a little something for you."

Out came an old soul as skinny as a fence rail. Ma went and offered her the collard greens and the rutabaga.

"Well, I do thank ye." The old woman was bright-eyed and spry-looking. She took what Ma offered. "I've been a-hankering for something like this the longest time! Now what can I do to help you?"

"To tell the truth, Granny," Ma began "I've come to see if you can tell me why Pa—that's Pa Puckett—can't ever raise a good crop of red peppers." And she went on to explain how puny his peppers turned out every year and how tasteless they were.

"Ma Puckett, I'm surprised you'd come all this way to ask me a thing like that," said the granny-witch. "It's so simple you ought to know it yourself."

Ma and the young'uns looked surprised.

"Pa Puckett's a mild man, ain't he?" Granny asked.

"He sure is," Ma said with pride. "He don't lose his temper

like a lot of men I know. He never goes a-feuding and shooting at his neighbors, no matter what they do. If they do him an
injury, he just forgives 'em. Oh, he's a mild-mannered man, all
right."

"There you are! That's the reason!" The granny-witch
bobbed her head up and down. "A man like that can't raise
hot peppers. They'll turn out just like he is every time, mild and
gentle. It takes a hot-tempered man to raise hot peppers; you
ought to know that."

"Well!" For a little spell Ma looked down, thoughtful-like.
She scuffed at the rocks with one foot. Then she looked up at
the witch-woman. "What can I do about it?"

"Come in," Granny beckoned to Ma with a skinny finger.
"Come in all by yourself and I'll put a flea in your ear."

Ma looked around at the young'uns, fearful-like. "You stay
right here," she whispered. "Wait till I come out. And if I
don't come out, you go get Pa and all the neighbors."

Then into the cave marched Ma behind the witch-woman.

The children stood there, holding onto each other and wondering if they would ever see their ma again. But pretty soon
here she came, smiling, safe and sound, and large as life. She
had a secret, knowing look on her face. The old granny-witch
came behind her, grinning and showing all her snaggled
teeth.

Ma thanked her and told her good-by, then she set off for
home with all the young'uns at her coat tails.

"What did she say, Ma?" the children begged. "Tell us
what she said. Did she give you a charm? Did she make a
witch-spell for Pa?"

"Never you mind," said Ma. "You'll find out soon enough.
Now just be quiet about this trip. Don't say a word to Pa, you
hear me? If you tell about it, I'll frazzle you out with a hickory
switch."

That night while they were eating their fried pork and corn pone, Pa sighed. "I'm a-going to plant the pepper crop to-morrow morning. We ought to get a real early start before the sun gets up. You better get things in order tonight, Ma, so's to have breakfast betimes tomorrow morning. And young-'uns, you go to bed early, so's you won't be too sleepy to turn out early in the morning. Maybe if we get those plants in real early so the hot sunshine doesn't get at 'em, the peppers will turn out better." He shook his head in a hopeless way as if he didn't really believe it would help.

That night after they were all asleep, Ma crept out of bed and made some preparations. She worked a while, very quietly, in the shed-room where they were all sleeping. Then she went into the kitchen and climbed on a chair. She worked there for quite a while. After that she went out onto the porch and thumped and thudded a while in the dark. Then she brushed her hands together, smiled to herself, and went back to bed.

The next morning Pa woke up with the earliest cockcrow. It was just getting light outside. He sat up in bed and sang out, "Ma! All you young'uns! Get up! Hurry now, we got to get an early start on those peppers."

He hopped out of bed in the half-dark and began to pull on his pants. He tried and tried to get his foot through the leg but it wouldn't go through.

"Now what's the matter here?" he cried.

The children sat up in bed. Their eyes were round with surprise as they watched Pa hopping and hopping around trying to make his foot go through his trouser-leg. When one foot wouldn't go, Pa tried the other, but that wouldn't go either. Then, while they watched, he sat down on the side of the bed and examined his pant-legs.

Somebody had tied a tight knot in the bottom of each leg.

"Now, young'uns." He looked reproachfully at the beds

where the children sat with popping eyes. "This is no time to be playing tricks. I haven't got time to be sitting here untying knots—"

"We didn't do it, Pa, honest Injun!" they cried.

"Well, get up now and make haste. We've got to get those peppers planted." Pa put his feet into his shoes and stood up. But when he started to walk off, his feet wouldn't move. He tried and tried but his feet wouldn't come off the floor.

"Now, what's the matter here?" Pa cried in alarm. "I can't get my feet offen the floor. I must be paralyzed!" There he stood, pulling and pulling, but his feet wouldn't come off the floor. "Lawsy, what's happened to me?"

The children were too amazed by Pa's strange actions to get out of bed. They just sat there staring at him straining to get his feet off the floor.

"Ma, Ma, wake up, something's happened to my feet!" Pa yelled.

Ma only grunted a little, like she was only half-awake.

Then of a sudden, one of Pa's feet came out of a shoe. His knee came up and gave him a blow on the chin.

"Ouch!" Pa clapped his hand to his chin. His other foot came out of the shoe and he went hopping around the room. "Golly, I'm not crippled after all!" he said with relief.

He got down on the floor and examined his shoes. Someone had nailed them to the floor, hard and tight.

"What are you up to?" he turned on the children. "You ought not to hold things up on a day like this, when I've laid off to plant the peppers." His voice was a little annoyed. "You ought to have more respect for your pa than to tie knots in his pants and nail his shoes to the floor."

The children looked at each other wide-eyed. "But, Pa, we didn't do it. We didn't know a thing about it!"

"You must have. Who else would do such pranks? You don't expect me to think your ma did such things, do you?"

Then he happened to notice that Ma wasn't up.

"Ma, Ma!" he called. "What's the matter? We've got to have an early breakfast, don't you remember?"

"M-mmm," mumbled Ma. "Don't bother me, I'm sleepy." She turned over in bed like she meant to have another hour there.

Pa didn't know what to think. Always before, Ma was the first one up.

"Ma, Ma, it's already sunup. We've got to get the peppers planted. Get up now and fix the breakfast." Pa shook her by the shoulder.

"I'm not a-going to cook any breakfast today!" Ma retorted angrily. "Get in there and cook your own breakfast if you want any."

"Wife, wife, are you sick?" exclaimed Pa. He had never seen Ma act like that.

"No, I'm not sick, but I'm tired of getting up and cooking breakfast every day of my life. Today I'm going to stay in bed and sleep. Now go along and leave me be."

Pa began to feel a little out of humor. It wasn't right of Ma to stay in bed on the particular day when the peppers had to be planted. He turned to the children.

"You get up right now before I upset the beds on top of you. If your ma won't go, somebody has to get out and help me plant the peppers."

The children hopped out of bed and hustled into their clothes while Pa untied the knots in his pants, pried his shoes away from the floor and got into them.

Pa peered out at the sun. "No time now to get breakfast," he said, "I'll just have a cup of coffee. That will have to do until dinnertime."

He went into the kitchen and blew on the coals. He looked in the coffee can. There was just enough coffee for one cup. He dumped it into the coffeepot and set the pot on the fire. Soon the coffee was bubbling. The whole cabin smelled good. Pa poured it into a cup and put in three heaping teaspoonsful of sugar.

"I sure need this," he said, "with everything in the house gone topsy-turvy. A good cup of coffee is a great help. Young-'uns, you can get yourselves some milk."

He blew in the cup and cooled the coffee a little. Then he took a good big swallow. Suddenly his eyes bugged out. His cheeks puffed out like a balloon.

The children, who had got themselves some milk from the pantry, stood and stared at him. What made Pa look so funny —just as if he was bit by a snake? While they stood watching, popeyed, Pa rushed to the front door. He blew the coffee all over the yard.

"I've a mind to give you a hiding!" Pa looked at them angrily. "And not a grain of coffee to make another cup!"

"What's the matter, Pa?" the children cried. "We didn't do anything. What's the matter with the coffee?"

"You know well enough." He picked up the sugar bowl and tasted. "Uh-huh, just as I thought. You've put salt in the sugar bowl!"

"We didn't do it, Pa, honest!" cried Mary.

"No, we didn't, Pa, honest!" exclaimed all the others.

"Hush up that talking! We've got to get going, just look how late it is. Come on now!" Pa unlatched the kitchen door and pushed it open.

As the door came open—slosh!—a bucket of cold water fell down all over Pa.

The children were too flabbergasted to move; they just stood looking.

"What—what?" stuttered Pa. He blew the water out of his nose, like a walrus. He wiped the drops out of his eyes. Then he looked up to see where all the water had come from. Someone had tied a bucket to a nail over the door. The bucket had been balanced on the top of the door so the first one to open it would upset it.

Suddenly the children began to giggle. Pa did look funny with his hair plastered down, dripping like a wet cat.

"Don't you laugh at me!" Pa yelled, "or I'll let you have it!"

The children put their hands over their mouths to muffle their snickers.

"You wait right here, while I change my clothes!" Pa shouted. "And no more tricks, I warn you!" He rushed into the house to put on dry clothes.

The young'uns waited on the porch. In a minute Pa came hurrying out. "Just look, the sun's already up! But I've laid off to plant those peppers and I mean to do it!" He strode across the porch and started down the steps. He didn't notice that the plank was removed from the bottom one. He put his foot down and the step wasn't there.

Crash! Down went Pa, flat on his face. There he lay sprawled on the path.

The children clapped their hands over their mouths but they couldn't keep from laughing.

"Ha, ha, ha, hee, hee! Hee, hee, hee!"

"So it's funny, huh!" Pa scrambled up. He snatched a switch from a peach tree beside the door. "I'll teach you to play pranks on me!" He charged at the children.

Ma stuck her head out the door, "Run, young 'uns, run!"

They sprinted away. Pa came after them, roaring. Mary ran one way, John went another. Alf flew toward the woods, Luli toward the fence. Every which way went Pa, grabbing at the flying children.

Ma came running to the edge of the field. "Now, now, Pa! Don't act up so!" she yelled. "That's no way to get the peppers planted. Just look, the sun is already high. In a little while it'll be hot enough to fry potatoes. The ground will be all dried out. The plants won't live."

At that Pa fetched up short. He was sweating and out of breath and he was mad clean through. But he couldn't catch the young'uns anyway, and after all, he *had* set out to plant the peppers.

"All right," he shouted. "We'll leave off this switching for now. But it's only long enough to get the peppers planted. After that you'll get what's coming to you!" He glared at Mary and John. He scowled at Alf and Luli. "You go get the hoes now and get at it."

So Pa and the children set to work, up one row they went and down another. Pa and Mary hoed up the ground. Alf and Luli dropped the plants and John followed behind hoeing the earth to firm it around the plants. The sun was hot, the children began to feel cross and out of humor. They hadn't had their breakfast. They were hungry and they all felt mean.

On they went, hoeing and dropping plants and hoeing again. On and on and on.

"I'm tired, Pa," whined Luli, "let's stop."

"I'm hungry," complained Alf. "Let's go get something to eat."

"It's too hot," said Mary. "I want to sit in the shade a while."

They whined and quarreled and snapped at each other.

"Shut up!" bawled Pa. He was the crossest of the lot. "I mean to keep on workng on this patch till every last row is planted."

At last, along toward dinnertime, it was done. The children sighed and laid down their hoes.

Pa straightened up. Well, it was done in spite of all. He began to feel better. Then—snuffle, snuffle, snout! He turned around.

There behind him all over the field was a drove of hogs. They were all busy, rooting up the rows of newly planted peppers.

"You—you—!" Pa choked. He raised his hoe and went charging at the hogs.

"Git—git out!" Pa struck right and left with his hoe but the hogs were too quick for him. They ran squealing up and down the rows looking for the way out, tearing up the newly planted field as they went. Up and down and all around ran the hogs, but they could not find the hole where they came in. The children ran, too, but they did more harm than good for they frightened the hogs more than ever so that they only ran squealing hither and yon.

After a while, here came Ma and headed the hogs to the open place where she had let them in. Out tumbled the hogs one on top of the other.

"Well!" Ma looked at Pa who was wet with sweat and red in the face. "You sure have made a mess of the pepper patch. Just look!" She waved her hand around at the field all trampled and cut to pieces.

"I?" Pa screamed at her. "I made a mess? Blame it on me will you, when you couldn't even get up to fix my breakfast. Well, now you can stay out here and help, tired or not! I'm a-going to plant this field today come hail or high water and you can stay and help me."

This was more than Ma had planned for. She hadn't had any breakfast either and working in the field wasn't woman's work. She started to give Pa a tart answer, but then she saw he was so worked up she was afraid to. Well, they set to again, all so mad they could hardly speak. They hoed up the rows and set the plants and hoed the earth around them again. And then, they shouldered their hoes and went back to the house.

Ma got out a cold pitcher of buttermilk. They all had some and felt better.

And how did those peppers finally turn out? Well, Pa Puckett set a record that year. He grew the hottest peppers ever seen or heard of in the mountains. The plants grew up most as high as his head. The peppers were so hot, folks didn't even dare to go into the pepper patch for fear of getting burned. When it rained, you could see the water sizzling when it fell on those peppers. It ran down the rows boiling up like it was poured outen the kettle. It scalded all the weeds right outen the patch. Pa never had to do any weeding. And when those peppers began to ripen, they smouldered and shone like chunks of red-hot iron. In the nighttime it was a sight to see 'em. The whole field was full of red lights. Folks came from all over to take a look.

When they were full-grown and ready to pick, it was a problem what to do about them. You couldn't touch one without getting burned to the bone. Finally, Pa thought of the fire tongs. He put on a pair of goggles, wrapped a wet quilt around him and brought the wheelbarrow. That's the way he harvested the peppers that year. And when thc sausages were finally madc in the wintertime, there never were such tasty red hot sausages.

"Next time," the young'uns said, gulping down cold water to keep from getting their throats burned, "we'd better let Pa get just half-mad. These peppers are just too much of a good thing!"

The Fighting Rams

"It was the queerest thing ever I saw," said Hank Huggins. "It was going on fifty years ago I saw it. I was hardly more than a young'un, driving a freight wagon from up in the hills down into the low country, but I ain't never forgot that contest and I never will. I heard it a long time before I saw it.

" 'Crash!' It sounded like two locomotives smashing head on. And then in a little while, 'Crash!' again.

"I was driving a pair of mules to a covered wagon, rolling through the pine woods with a load of ginseng root—a mighty valuable cargo. Digging ginseng root was a good way of making money in those days. A body could take a shovel and range through the woods in the mountains and find it growing just anywhere. There in the shade among the ferns, you'd spy those pointed green leaves growing outen a knobby sort of bulb. You'd dig it up and it was just like picking up five dollars outen a pig's track. Nowadays you can't find nary a sign of ginseng no matter how you search. It's been cleaned outen the woods, dug up, every smidgen of it.

"Well, there I was driving through the pine woods with a load of that costly root. When I heard all that clanging and clattering up ahead it made me feel a mite skittish. I didn't know what it was. I couldn't even guess. And I began to think

82

of all the tales I'd heard of holdups in the woods. A gang of robbers would jump outen the bushes all of a sudden, make away with the driver, and take his wagon with all the goods. I halted there in the woods, listening and trying to figure out what it could be.

" 'Clang!' would go this noise. Silence for about five minutes, then, 'Bong!'

"No, it wouldn't be robbers, I decided. Robbers wouldn't make a sound. You wouldn't know they were around until they were right on top of you. Well, lingering there in the woods wasn't any way to find out. And whatever it was, it probably wasn't anything that would bother me. So I clucked to the mules and drove on.

"I began to see the sunlight through the trees and then I came out onto a meadow, pretty and green, with a little stream flowing through it. At first I didn't see anything unusual—just a flock of sheep standing there on the grass. Then I noticed something queer. Those sheep were hardly moving a muscle. They were just standing, all looking in one direction. Then I saw there were two flocks of sheep. One flock was white.

Every sheep in it was white. Those in the other flock were black—every last one of 'em, as black as soot. There they were, those two flocks of sheep standing facing each other, something like two armies drawn up ready for a battle. There was a great big space out there in the middle between the two flocks.

"And then I spied what was making all the racket. Two big rams—one white, t'other one black—were tearing around out there in that space. They were both snorting mad and by the looks of them they'd laid off to fight something out to the finish. What it was they were fighting about I don't know. Maybe they both wanted to be kingpin of the two flocks. Maybe they were both in love with the same beautiful lady sheep. Whatever it was, they were riled up about it and meant to battle it out then and there.

"I pulled the mules to a stop and sat there watching. Those old bucks would back off three or four yards and then they'd run at each other, heads lowered, as fast as they could pelt.

" 'Wham!' their horns would crash together. Seems like everything around would tremble with that smash. The black flock would jostle a little, like they'd been struck, then they'd stretch their necks to see what had happened. And the white flock would do the same. It just seemed to me like that crash ought to knock those rams unconscious. No, sir! they'd shake their heads a bit to settle their brains back in place, then they'd back off and go at it again.

"I sat there watching for an hour or two and they never paused, neither the black one nor the white one. Over and over they'd back off, and then go at each other head-on. The two flocks just stood there watching, craning their necks to see if maybe one of 'em would knock the other out. But each was about as strong as t'other and neither one showed any sign of getting tired.

"I wanted to stick around and see what would happen in the

end, but ginseng root loses weight as it dries up. If I waited too long I'd lose money. I had to get my load down to Charleston, and have it weighed and sell it while it was plump and heavy. I was sorry to leave before the battle was settled, but I clucked to the mules and drove on. For quite a spell the sound of those two rams a-meeting head-on followed me down the road.

"Well, I got to Charleston about a week later. I sold my ginseng root and saw it off on a ship headed for China. There's where most of the stuff went. The Chinese used it for medicine, so they said. Then I bought my return load—coffee, salt, such things as we didn't make ourselves up in the mountains—and headed for home.

"When I got near that meadow where the two rams had been fighting I began to wonder how that contest had turned out. I wondered what I'd find when I got there. It would be settled one way or another, I was sure. But as I got near the place I began to hear a dull thumping. 'Thud!' it would sound. Then after a little spell, 'Thump!'

" 'For the land's sake, it can't be they're still at it,' I said to myself. I touched up the mules and hurried on. When I got in sight of that meadow, what did I see but those two old rams going for each other just like they had two weeks ago. They were a mite slower than when I came past, but they hadn't given up, not by a long sight. No, sir! But their horns were gone. They'd worn 'em clean down to nothing with their butting and butting away. But that hadn't discouraged them none. There they were backing off and running at each other and thumping their bare heads together. You would have thought they would addle their brains the way they came at each other head-on and bumped their skulls together. But no, they'd stagger a little each time, then they'd back off and go for each other again.

"The two flocks had lost interest. The white flock was grazing around on the same side with the white ram, and the black flock was over behind the black ram, but they were nibbling away on the grass not paying too much attention to the battle. Only once in a while one would lift his head and look toward his leader fighting there on the grass.

"Well, I stayed a while, watching, and then I drove on. As I pulled up into the mountains I kept thinking of the two old rams. When were they going to give up and call it quits? When I got high enough to peer over the trees down into the valley I looked to see if I could pick out that meadow and get a glimpse of the two critters to find out if they were still butting each other. But it seems like there were a lot of meadows down there and they were so far away I couldn't tell which was which, much less make out any sheep.

"I finally got back up here to the mountains and turned over my goods to the storekeeper. Then I went on home to rest up a spell. I still had those battling sheep on my mind, and seems like I was glad when the storekeeper sent word that he had another load of ginseng to go down to the coast. I could hardly wait to get down to that meadow to see how that fight had been settled.

"When I got into the pinewoods where I'd first heard the banging and clanging, I turned my head this way and that trying to hear if the battle was still going on. But no, all was quiet.

" 'Sure enough, they've given it up,' I said to myself. I drove outen the woods and looked around. There were the two flocks of sheep, all right. The white flock was grazing in the upper part of the meadow as peaceful as you please. At its head was the white ram, grazing with them, throwing up its head now and then and looking around in a watchful way. The black ram was leading the black herd down in the lower meadow. I was surprised considerable.

" 'The old boys have settled their differences!' I said to myself.

"Then I looked again. The two rams each had a fine set of horns. Now that couldn't be! Those fighting fellows had worn off their horns. They couldn't have grown another set. No, sir! Then I caught on. They were different rams, those fellows out there now. They were young ones and they had taken the places of those two that had been out there butting and butting each other for so many days.

"Now what could have become of the two old fighters? It was a puzzle. I stopped the mules and sat there looking every which way to see if I could find any sign of 'em.

"Then out in the middle of that meadow I caught sight of something queer. Never in all my days had I seen anything queerer. Something white and fluffy was out there blowing back and forth, a little above the ground. It was right over the place where the white ram had run back and forth to butt the black one. I could tell because the ground was cut up and the grass all worn away. Then, on the other side, I caught sight of something fuzzy and black. It was flying back and forth where the black ram had been.

"I put my hand up to shade my eyes and peered closer. Then I understood. They were sheeps' tails out there flying at each other. They'd back off a few yards, the white one and the black one, then they'd rush at each other and bounce together there in the middle of the meadow. Then they'd float away from each other; they'd pause a minute and then they'd fly together again.

"Well, sir, if it wasn't the darnedest thing! It was all that was left of those two stubborn old rams. They'd kept at it until they'd worn themselves clean down to their tails. And still they wouldn't give up.

"And while I sat there a-watching, the two tails wore away, every hair. Not a thing was left of 'em. Those two obstinate critters had butted and butted themselves smack to nothing.

"Well, sir, I drove on thinking it over. 'Now there's a lesson,' I said to myself, 'if you want to take it.' What was the lesson? Well, folks, think hard. Figure it out for yourselves."

The Self-Kicking Machine

Young Clint Dowling was as brainy a young'un as ever was born on Skin-shin Ridge. His mammy and pappy were proud of him a sight. He was hardly dry behind the ears before they decided they ought to send him off to college. So off he went. He stayed four years and came back with a head full of knowledge. Whatever kind of work a body set out to do, Clint could tell him how to do it. Oh, he was full of brainy ideas, though he was never a one to do any work himself.

One day he came into the cabin where his ma was churning. There she was working the dasher up and down, up and down to make the butter come.

"Now, Mammy, how come you don't think of a quicker way of doing that?" Clint asked. "Look how much time you spend every day a-working that dasher up and down, up and down. You might be using your time for something else."

"What other way is there?" asked Mammy. "I skim the cream off the top of the milk. I pour it into the churn, then I work the dasher up and down, up and down, until the cream turns to butter. It's the way my mammy did it in her time and my old granny before her. What other way is there?"

"Use your head, use your head. There are always means of saving yourself work," said Clint.

"If there's another way, you find it, Mr. Smart-Alec!" said his mammy who had got a little tired of being told how to do her work.

"Leave it to me," said Clint. "Tomorrow just you put the cream into the churn and I'll see that it's churned without lifting a hand."

His mammy took Clint at his word. On the following day she poured the cream in the churn and told him he was welcome to figure out how to get it churned without effort. And away she went to the vegetable garden to cut some turnip greens to cook with their salt pork in the black pot in the chimney.

When she got back with her apron full of greens, what was her amazement to see the churn sitting there in the middle of the floor splishing and splashing all by itself. No one was near it and the dasher hung on the wall where she had left it the day before. It was mighty curious. She ran to open the top to see what could be happening inside the churn.

"No, no, don't touch it!" cried young Clint. "When the splishing and the splashing stop, that will be time enough to open the churn. Then you'll know the butter has come. Just call me. I'll open the churn for you." And he went out to watch his pappy feed and water the horse.

Ma Dowling was greatly mystified. She swept the floor and washed the dishes and all the while the splishing and splashing went on inside the churn. The poor woman was half dead with curiosity. She could hardly get her work done for wondering what was making the churn go all by itself. At last it just seemed like she couldn't stand it a minute longer.

"I'll just have one little peep. What harm can that do? Clint will never know a thing about it." She tiptoed to the churn, leaned over it, and lifted the lid.

Then she fell back with a yelp. Three big green bullfrogs

leaped up into her face. Sping-spang-sping! They were covered with cream and went leaping and plopping about all over the cabin.

"Oh, help, help!" Mammy ran after them, grabbing at the air as they jumped this way and that. "They're spattering cream on everything!"

Pappy and Clint came on the run. What a sight! Those frogs were jumping every which way—onto the bed, into the flour barrel, onto the table. Oh, the air was full of frogs!

"Oh, my nice, neat cabin!" wailed Mammy. "It'll never come clean again!"

What a time they had catching those greasy frogs. Pappy grabbed one, but it slipped out of his hand and went hopping under the bed. Then Clint got one, but it oozed out of his grasp and gave a leap onto the mantelpiece. When at last they were all cornered and caught, Mammy and Pappy and Clint were out of breath and the cabin was full of cream from one end to the other.

"You and your bright ideas!" Mammy said to Clint. "Look what trouble they've caused!"

"It was your own fault, Mammy," Clint told her. "I told you not to open the churn. I meant to take it down to the brook, open it there and let the frogs jump into the water. Then no harm would have been done."

"Humph! Even if the frogs hadn't escaped, the butter would have been ruined. Who would eat it after those dirty frogs had been jumping around in it?"

"How could the frogs be dirty," asked Clint, "when they've spent their whole lives bathing in the clean brook water?"

For an answer Mammy lifted the churn and dumped the rest of the cream into the hogs' bucket.

Pappy and Clint went back to the barn. Pappy sat down on a stool to milk the cow, and Clint stood by to give him advice.

Flies were swarming in the cow stall and Bossy was plagued with their biting. She kept swinging her tail to keep them away. Every time she gave it a fling, it slapped Pappy across the face. He was pestered half to death. He bawled at the cow, he threatened, and he blustered.

"Now, Pappy," Clint reproved him. "You're not doing any good shouting and bellowing like that. Why don't you use your head? Think up some way to keep the cow from switching her tail."

"Think up a way yourself, if you're so smart," said Pappy angrily.

"It's as easy as falling off a log," said Clint. "Tie the cow's tail to your leg and then she can't swing it."

"Humph!" Pappy didn't look up. He was in no mood to try out any of Clint's brainy ideas. But the cow kept slapping and slapping him until he was plagued past endurance. "Dog take it, anything is better than this!" He got up and tied the cow's tail to his bootstrap.

Without the use of her tail, poor Bossy was maddened by the flies. She shook herself, she fidgeted, and flinched, but she could not unsettle those biting flies. She shivered and quivered her hide but they bit all the harder. Finally a big horsefly lit and stung her on the back. It was more than flesh and blood could bear. She upped with her foot and kicked right and left. The milk bucket went flying and the milk was spilled all over the stall.

"You ding-busted critter!" Pappy lost his temper. He jumped up and gave Bossy a hard kick in the ribs. He forget about being tied to her tail.

Bossy gave a leap. It snatched Pappy's leg from under him.

What a to-do! "Whoa, there, whoa!" roared Pappy. This frightened Bossy all the more. She ran out of the stable, mooing with fright, and dragged Pappy all over the farmyard. There she went, bellowing and mooing, with poor Pap bumping and thumping behind.

Mammy and Clint went running to catch her. By the time they had her cornered and quieted, poor Pappy was battered and bruised.

"What in the land o' living made you tie the cow's tail to your bootstrap?" cried Mammy as she bent to untie him. "What a silly thing to do!"

"It was that brainy son of yours," bellowed Pappy. "It was his bright idea and I'm half killed by it. I could kick myself for sending him to college."

"And I need a kicking for agreeing to it," Mammy said.

"Ah-ha, that gives me a bright idea!" exclaimed Clint.

"I'll have nothing to do with any more bright ideas." Pappy hobbled into the house.

"Nor I," agreed Mammy. And she followed him inside.

And so Clint was left alone to carry out his idea if he cared to. He got a hammer and a saw, a log, a board, and some nails. Then he set to work. All day long he was banging and scraping away.

"What are you making?" Mammy stuck her head out of the door to ask.

"All in good time, all in good time," Clint held up his palm at her.

In the late afternoon Clint called his mammy and pappy. His work was completed. There in the yard stood a strange contraption. A board was fastened over a log like a seesaw. On one end a wooden leg stuck up with an old shoe on it. Mammy and Pappy started at it in perplexity. Whatever could it be?

"Stand here," Clint said to Pap. "Bend over a little and stamp on the end of the board."

Pappy changed places with Clint. He gave a hard stamp

on the end of the board. Up came the shoe and gave him a hard kick in the rear.

"Ouch!" yelled Pappy. "It kicked me!"

"You kicked yourself," corrected Clint.

"So I did!" said Pappy, greatly surprised.

"Now it's my turn," Mammy stepped in front of the contraption and stamped on the board. "Ouch!" she yelled.

Word of the self-kicking machine got around. And as it turned out, there were a lot of people on Skin-shin Ridge who felt like kicking themselves. So many people came to use the machine that Clint got the bright idea of charging a quarter a kick.

The money began to pile up. Mammy bought a new kitchen stove and a new flowered hat. Pappy got a cultivator and a good strong mule to pull it. Things began to look up.

"After all," they finally agreed. "The college education *was* worth while."

The Lake That Flew

Hank Huggins sat atop a zigzag rail fence, enjoying the fine spring weather.

"Howdy, Hank!" a passing neighbor greeted him. "Pretty day, isn't it? Reckon we'll have a spell of fine weather now."

"I wouldn't lay any bets on that," said Hank, casting a doubtful eye over the panorama of Blue Ridge Mountains. "You never can tell what the weather's going to do in these hills. Do you remember what happened to me that time I went out shooting geese on Dishpan Lake?"

"Can't say as I do."

"Queerest thing you ever heard tell of," Hank said. "It was in the fall of the year it happened, when the wild geese were a-flying over on their way south. About dusk one night I noticed a big flock settle down on the lake. It was too dark then to get a good shot at 'em, but I made up my mind to get up early and be on hand at sunrise to pick off a few when they took off. A nice roast goose would go mighty good, I thought.

"Well, sir, I was up betimes, just as I'd laid off to be. It was nice weather for fall, not too hot and not too cold, and it didn't show any sign of changing. But let me tell you it did change, and that in a hurry. The wind shifted, clouds whirled over the peaks, and before I knew what was happening, it was way down below freezing. I could feel the grass crunching and crackling under my feet. The bushes and brambles were as brittle as glass. The dew on 'em had turned to ice. Everything was frozen stiff. I was pretty cold myself and hustled along as fast as I could, to keep my blood warm.

"I got to the lake about sunup. What I saw there surprised me considerable. There were the geese all right, a big flock of 'em, but such a gabbling and honking I never heard in all my life. They were mighty upset about something, I could tell that. And the way they were acting wasn't natural. One would flap his wings as hard as he could, as if he meant to take to the air, but he never moved a mite. Then another would try it, and another and another.

"I stood there on the bank for a spell, wondering what in all get-out was the matter. Then it came to me what must have happened. The lake had frozen over suddenly while those geese were asleep. It had caught their legs tight in the ice, and now the geese were stuck like flies on flypaper.

" 'Jumping Jehoshaphat!' I said to myself. 'What a piece of luck. Those geese can't get away. I can walk right out there on that ice and knock off enough to last me a year. It won't even cost me a gun shell.'

"I tried the ice to see if it would hold my weight. It was as hard as a rock, so I strode out toward a big gander and hauled off with my gun to knock him on the head. But it wasn't going to be as easy as I thought. That fellow had a mighty long wingspread. He fought at me, slapping me in the face, knocking off my hat, and batting the gun clean out of my hands. I saw I'd have to shoot him, so I backed off a little, took aim, and fired.

"Well, sir, the report of that gun roared over that lake like a thunderclap. It frightened those geese half outen their wits and every pair of wings beat the air at once. At the same moment, from all around the edges of the lake, there came a loud cracking sound. Then I felt the ice a-moving under my feet. I didn't know what to make of it. It was going up—up —up into the air. Before I could get my wits together, I found myself up above the treetops. Those geese, exerting themselves all at once, had lifted that frozen lake right out of its bed. They were flying away with it and with me, too, for I was standing right in the middle of it.

"I never was in such a predicament in my life. When I looked down I near about had heart failure. There below was the steeple of the Baptist church. My house was nearby, looking no bigger than a matchbox and getting smaller every minute.

" 'Jumping Jehoshaphat! How am I going to get down from here?' I said to myself. It was too late to jump, that was certain. I told myself I'd better make the best of it and stay right

there till the geese got in the notion to make a landing. They'd have to settle down at nightfall for sure. But then it came to me that we were heading south, toward warm weather. It wouldn't be long before that ice would begin to melt—and then what? I began to study what I could do to get out of that fix.

"If I upped with my gun and killed off the geese with two or three shots, the lake would fall and I'd be cracked to pieces, just like the ice. Then I had a bright idea. It was what finally solved the problem and saved my life. I took aim with my gun and shot one goose. The lake dropped just a mite nearer the ground. In a minute I shot another goose. Down sank the lake by a foot or two more. Well, sir, I kept that up, knocking off one goose at a time until we were only a few feet from the ground. By that time there were only six or seven big ganders left and they were so winded they gave up, one by one, and we dropped down as gently as landing on a featherbed. It was just in time, too, for the sun had got mighty hot.

"I waited around until the last of that lake melted away, and then I gathered up the geese. There was a pile of 'em as high as a haystack, and I had to hire a wagon to carry 'em all home.

"My wife was a mite surprised to see what a load I had. She said, 'For the land's sake, Hank! You sure were lucky to bring these geese down.'

" 'Honey,' I said to her, 'I was still luckier to bring myself down.' "

The Man Who Rode the Bear

Back in the times when the Indians were still a-raiding around in the Blue Ridge Mountains, there was an old bear that had the people more scarified than the Indians ever did. He was a terror—as big as a horse, people said, and ferocious, too. It seemed like a bullet didn't even tickle him. If he was hit, he'd just shake himself and go right on about his business. He raided pigpens, carried off sheep, and wasn't even afraid to hang around the cabins at night and take a grab at anybody that came out. It got so folks were afraid to be out after dark.

Well, the critter went over to Sowback Ridge one night and got into the pigpen of a fellow named Joe Dowdy. Joe and his wife Tildy didn't hear a sound. It was raining and they were moving the furniture here and there to keep the rain from wetting it. Their old roof leaked like a sieve, and no sooner did they get the bed moved away from a place where the water was coming through than they would hear a drip, drip on something else. What with all the noise they made, dragging the bed and the chest and the table around, and with the rain beating down on the shingles overhead, they never heard their hog a-squealing.

The bear killed the pig and dragged him around behind the

barn. There he made a meal of him, hair, hide, and hoof. Then, gorged with his meal, the bear lay down under the eaves of the barn, where he was protected from the rain, and went to sleep.

It was too bad about Joe's hog because it was his last one, all he and Tildy had to provide meat for the winter. Joe was the kind of man that seemed born for bad luck. If he planted a corn patch, there would be rain all around the country but never a drop in his field. His neighbors' corn would grow tall and green, and Joe's would burn up for lack of water. His livestock were always dying off with one thing or another, and it seemed he just couldn't get ahead.

Tildy didn't have any better luck than her husband. Foxes caught her chickens, and her turkeys got lost in the woods. So it went until the night the bear paid them a visit. By that time Joe and Tildy had nothing in the world but the leaky cabin, the hog, and a poor decrepit old horse. And now, though they didn't know it, their hog was inside the bear.

Along about four o'clock in the morning, when the rain let

up a little, Joe and Tildy sat down in front of the fireplace
and began to talk about their situation.

"If I could only get the reward they're offering for that old
bear, it would put us on Easy Street," Joe said. "It's a lot of
money. I might just try it."

"Oh, talk sense," said Tildy impatiently. "Everybody in
the mountains has tried it. Folks have gone in bands to get
him. He's clawed Jake Sadler and raked open Solly Sneed.
He just about chewed an arm offen Sam Tolan. He's killed
so many dogs there's hardly any left to chase rabbits. Everybody's scared for their lives of that critter. Do you think you
can go out and bring him in all by your lonesome?"

"Well—" Joe hung his head.

"And what would you hunt him with?" Tildy went on.
"Your gun has been sold these three months. Nobody would
lend you his, not with that bear likely to show up anywhere.
Are you aiming to go out and get him with your bare hands?"

Joe sighed.

"You'd better think of looking for work," said Tildy. "I
heard yesterday that the miller down the creek a piece is
looking for a man to help with the grinding. Why don't you
get down there and ask for the job?"

"I've got no more chance of getting that job than I have
of killing the bear," said old Joe. "There're a dozen younger
men that want it."

"Oh, don't be so chickenhearted!" exclaimed Tildy. "If
you're the first one there in the morning, like as not you'll get
it."

"Well," said Joe doubtfully, "I reckon it wouldn't hurt to
try."

"Wouldn't hurt to try!" echoed Tildy. "Well, I reckon it
wouldn't. Get out right now and saddle up the horse and get
along."

"Why, it's dark now," said Joe, "I couldn't see to saddle the horse."

"Get along. You'll manage with the horse; do it by the feel. Day will be breaking an hour from now and the miller will be ready to pick his man and get on with the grinding. You be there! If you get there an hour early, it won't hurt."

Well, Joe got up, clamped some spurs on his boots—for his poor old horse needed plenty of urging—and put on his coat.

Then he had a thought. He turned to Tildy. "It's dark as Egypt outside. S'posen that old bear should be hanging round here."

"Oh shucks, that bear is miles away. He got a calf over at Alf Heeney's place last night. That's a good fifteen miles from here."

"That's a far piece, for sure. I reckon it's safe enough to go out."

With that Joe said good-by and walked out to the barn. It had stopped raining but the clouds still hung low. Not a star could be seen, and Joe couldn't make out a thing in the dark. He found the barn easy enough for he knew every stone on the path. He felt his way to the place where he kept his saddle and bridle, and took them off the peg. Then he made his way to the stall where the horse slept. He held out his hands and walked this way and that inside the stall, but he couldn't find the horse. He wasn't in his stall, and that was queer; animals don't like being outside on a rainy night. The fact was that the horse had smelled the bear and had run clean away to the woods.

"Now where's that horse?" said Joe. He went outside and stumbled here and there, feeling along the fences and around the well. Then he went back to the barn and felt along the walls. At the back, he stumbled over the bear lying under the eaves sound asleep.

Joe put out his hand and felt the hair on the bear's neck. "Oh, so there you are, you crazy critter!" He grabbed the bear by the ear. "Haven't you got enough sense to stay in outen the rain?"

Well, the bear was so logy with a whole hog in his stomach that he didn't even wake up. While he snored away, Joe opened his mouth and put the bit in; he buckled the bridle on his head. He threw the saddle across the bear's back and then gave him a kick in the ribs.

"Get up, you no-count critter! Let me fasten this bellyband."

The bear roused himself groggily, and hoisted himself onto his feet. Joe quickly fastened the bellyband. Then he leaped into the saddle. He gave the critter a jab with his spurs.

That bear woke up for sure. He felt the thing tied around his middle and the load on his back. He gave himself a terrific shake. It almost threw poor old Joe from the saddle. "What's the matter with you?" he cried, and he beat the bear's head with the handle of his whip.

The bear had never had anything like this happen to him. He reached around to claw Joe off his back, but his arms wouldn't reach. He couldn't get his head back that far to bite. And all the time Joe was beating him about the ears with the handle of the whip and sticking him with his spurs.

"Get up there, get!" Joe yelled. The night was so black that he never had an idea what it was he was contending with.

That old bear was scarified outen his wits. He took off down the road as fast as he could gallop. Every now and then he'd hump himself and jump up in the air, trying to throw off whatever it was that had him around the middle. Never in his life had Joe had such a ride. Who would have thought the old horse had it in him? he wondered.

It was a good seven miles to the mill and that bear ran every step of the way. By the time he got there he was run

near to death. He was so tuckered out that when Joe pulled up on the reins to stop him, he just stood swaying, with his tongue hanging out and all the fight out of him.

In the dark, Joe threw the halter rope around the hitching post and tied it. Then he sat down on the steps of the mill to wait till the miller appeared.

It wasn't long before the sunrise began to lighten the sky and the day came on. The miller entered his mill through the back door and unlocked the front one, ready to do business. He saw Joe leaning against the wall.

"Good morning, Joe Dowdy. Have you come for some meal? How'd you get here so early?"

"I rode," said Joe, pointing with his thumb over his shoulder. "There's my horse out there tied to the hitching post."

The miller looked. His eyes popped half out of his head. He tottered backward. There stood the bear, saddled and bridled and tied to the hitching post.

"You—rode—that?" squalled the miller.

"Sure," said Joe without turning around. "Why not?"

The miller gulped and stuttered. He looked at Joe as though he'd never seen him before. He'd never thought Joe Dowdy was much of a man—but there was the bear. The very bear that had been terrorizing the whole settlement. And here was Joe acting as though bear-taming was nothing at all.

"I came to see you about that j-job." Joe stuttered a little. "I'd admire to have it, if you ain't got a man no better."

"B-b-better!" stammered the miller. "Where would I find a better man than you? You can have the job, and welcome."

By that time folks had begun to arrive with their meal to be ground. When they saw the bear tied to the hitching post, they were struck dumb with astonishment. They forgot all about taking their meal into the mill. At first, they just stood; then they began carrying on—exclaiming and asking questions.

"Who—who rode him?" They stared at the bear and then at the miller.

"Joe, here, rode him up just before daybreak."

Joe turned around then, to see what all the commotion was about. When he saw the bear, his eyes flew open. His heart almost stopped. He was so shocked that the breath went out of him and he couldn't say a word.

"Well, Joe, you're the man that gets the reward!" the miller said. "You sure have earned it. Tell us—how did you manage it?"

Joe was so scarified to think what he'd done that he could only gasp, "I—I'd ruther not talk about it."

Well, the fame of old Joe Dowdy went all over the mountains. Such a stouthearted fellow there'd never been since the land was settled. The money for capturing the bear came in mighty handy for Joe and Tildy. They put a new roof on their house, bought themselves a cow, several hogs, and some poultry. So now they were well off. But if Joe thought he could settle down and enjoy his good fortune, he had another think a-coming.

When the time came to elect a sheriff, it was only natural that folks should think of Joe. All the mountain men met at the crossroads store and they agreed that he was the man for the job. There were some pretty tough horse thieves about; robbers appeared now and then, and sometimes rowdy fellows got to fighting with knives. Yes, Joe could handle them if anybody could.

The very thought of the sheriff's duties gave Joe the cold shivers. But he decided he'd better not refuse until he had talked it over with Tildy. "Let me think it over a bit," he told the men. "Being sheriff is a mighty big responsibility. I'll let you know about it tomorrow morning."

Joe set out for home. When he got there he explained to

Tildy all that had happened. Tildy listened and looked thought-ful.

"They pay the sheriff a mighty big salary," she said. "You'd better take the job. You know the sheriff has a man to help him out. A deputy, they call him. If anything dangerous turns up, you can send him to handle it, while you stay out of harm's way and direct things."

Well, that solved the problem. Joe went back to the store the next day and accepted the job.

They gave Joe a big husky fellow for a deputy. If Joe didn't appear to take care of some ruffian, people said it was a job not worthy of a man like Joe. He'd just as well save him-self for something big. So everything went all right for a year or two. Then there was a serious problem for old Joe Dowdy.

Word got around that the Indians were acting up again. They were going on the warpath by the looks of things, and all through the mountains people were worried. The men of the community got together at the store to see what could be done about it. They were all there but Joe, who had found an excuse to stay home.

"We'll have to get together and fight 'em," said Solly Sneed. "There's no other way."

"How can we fight 'em?" Jake Jones wanted to know. "There are maybe two hundred of them and only fifty of us."

"They're a-gathering," said the miller. "Whilst we chew the rag, they're a-sharpening their war hatchets."

"Within a week they'll be on us!" shouted Sam Cobble.

"Let's call on Joe Dowdy; he'll get us out of this!" someone cried.

"Sure, sure, we'll call on Joe. Why didn't we think of that before?"

Everybody gave a sigh of relief. Yes, Joe was the man to save the day.

So a messenger was sent to tell Joe they were all depending on him. He should put his mind to it, and save them from the Indians. It hardly needs saying that Joe was scared outen his wits.

"Why, Bud," he said to the messenger, "how can I do that?"

"Any way it suits you, Joe," Bud replied. "We know you can take care of twenty or thirty Indians by yourself. Maybe we fellows could handle the rest. While you're getting your coat, I'll go out and saddle your horse for you." And he set off for the barn.

Joe rushed into the house. "Tildy! Tildy!" he shouted.

Tildy came running. "What now?"

Joe poured out the story of what had happened. "Fight twenty or thirty Indians all by my lonesome! What'll I do? I think I had just better go and explain how that business about catching the bear was all a misunderstanding. I'll make 'em see that I ain't a mite braver than anyone else."

"Wait!" said Tildy. "If you do that, you'll lose your job as sheriff, and then where will we be? We've got used to having money now, and it would be mighty hard to be poor again."

"But what can I do? Bud's out there now, a-saddling my horse."

"Let me think," Tildy told him. She sat with her head in her hands. "Well," she said at last, "you might stall just a little and gain some time. Go over to the store and tell the men that you'll have to take a couple of days to scout out the situation, to see where the Indians are camped and how many there are. Say you want to spy out their plans.

"You wouldn't really have to go near the Indians. You could just ride over that-a-way. Let folks think you're a-going. Then you can hide in the woods a day or so, and come on home with some tale to satisfy them. Meanwhile, I'll be thinking up some excuse to get us out of this fix."

Since there seemed nothing else to do, Joe decided to take his wife's advice. He went out and mounted his old nag and rode with the messenger down to the store. He said to the gathering just what Tildy had told him to. They all agreed it was a sensible plan.

"But you ought not to go on a horse like that," the miller said. "That old bag of bones can hardly get into a trot. If some Indians were to ride after you, they'd overhaul you in no time. We'll get you a good horse."

"He can have mine," spoke up Solly Sneed. "I reckon he can outrun anything! Of course, he's a mite hard to handle, but anybody that could saddle up a bear and ride it ought to be able to manage my horse."

Now everybody in the mountains knew Solly's horse. He was a half-wild brute of a critter that only Solly could ride. He'd buck and bite, and he'd run fit to throw the old Boogerman himself. The thought of getting on his back scared Joe almost as much as facing the Indians. But there was nothing for it but to accept Solly's offer.

"Well, I'll just ride my old horse home," Joe said, "and get some grub. I'll lead Sol's horse on behind, and he'll be there ready to mount after I've fixed up something to eat."

The men all agreed that this was a good idea. "We'll stay here at the store to wish you good luck as you go by," they said.

Home went poor Joe, feeling that his last day had come for sure. He showed Tildy the horse. "I'll never stay on his back a minute," he said. "He'll hump me off like I was a rabbit. Then he'll trample me, just outen spite. And the men all waiting at the store to see me go by!"

"Oh my!" cried Tildy, "what shall we do?" And she put

her head in her hands, to think. In a few minutes she came up with a plan.

"We'll feed him some corn," she said, "and while he's eating I can tie your feet under his stomach. That way he can't buck you off. You ride by the store, then circle around the woods and come back home. You can hide in the barn loft a few days until it's time to report to the men at the store."

Joe wasn't too pleased with the idea of being tied onto the horse, but there seemed to be no other way out of his predicament. So they fed the horse a big helping of corn and, while he was munching it, Joe mounted and Tildy tied his feet with a rope under the horse's belly.

Joe set off easily enough. The horse was full of corn and in no mood for acting up. But when they came to the store, Joe kicked him in the ribs. If he passed the store at a fast clip, he thought, the fellows wouldn't see that his feet were tied. Well, kicking that horse was a mighty rash act, and Joe soon found it out. The critter let out a whinny and hoisted himself up on his hind legs. Then he set off for other places. Joe whizzed by the store like he was shot out of a cannon. The men hardly saw him before he was out of sight.

Joe couldn't stop that horse to save his life. He pulled and he sawed, but the animal took the bit in his teeth and went streaking on. The worst of it was, he was headed right for the Indian camp.

Now the Indians had set guards along the road to warn them in case the whites should attack. Two fellows were close in and two farther on down the road.

As Joe came abreast of the first two, they leaped out in all their war paint. They tried to stop the horse. One seized the bridle, the other tried to grab the saddle. But lawsy! They didn't have a chance. That horse upped with his back feet and kicked one Indian half a mile down the road. He reached around with his teeth and took a bite out of the other one. The fellow squalled and jumped back. The horse humped himself and galloped on.

"Here comes a white man!" the Indian bawled to the guards closer in. "Even his horse is trained to fight. He kicks with his heels and bites with his teeth. He kicked my partner and cracked his skull. He pretty near bit my arm off!"

The near guards were scared a sight. They bellowed on to the camp: "Here come the white men! Their horses are worse fighters than the men. They thrash with their hoofs and crack people's skulls; they bite off arms with their teeth!"

This news set the Indian camp in an uproar. Everybody was running around telling the news to everybody else, and with every telling the tale got bigger. Such horses had never been heard of. How could they defend themselves against an army of such terrible critters?

Meanwhile, the horse thundered on. But with all the kicking he had done, and the humping and running, the rope that tied Joe's feet began to work loose. Joe knew he'd have a terrible fall if it came untied. How could he save himself? I'll grab a tree limb over the road, he thought, and haul myself offen this hog-wild critter.

He reached out to grab the first tree he came near. It was small and had hardly any roots. It came out in his hand and there he went, galloping past the second set of guards brandishing a tree torn up by the roots.

"Here come the white men!" the guards shouted. "They pull up trees by the roots without getting outen their saddles. Here they come, a-shaking them over their heads for war clubs!"

This news struck terror into the whole Indian camp. Men that pulled up trees by the roots. Horses that bit off arms and legs and cracked people's skulls. It was death to stay and face such monsters! Like a swarm of locusts, the Indians fled out of camp and took to the woods. When Joe and the horse came charging in among the tents, not a red man was left.

Joe hadn't thought to drop the tree, and it was banging and beating against the horse's side. It set the critter wild for sure. He charged around, kicking and bucking. He knocked down teepees, kicked over cooking pots, and trampled the Indians' belongings. There was never such havoc created by a horse before. That finished off the job of loosening Joe's feet, but he still stuck on. It was better than falling.

From behind the trees the Indians saw all the rampaging. The chief yelled for his counselors. "We'd better send him a peace pipe," he cried, "before the rest of 'em get here!"

"Send him a pipe!" the counselors agreed at once.

By the time Joe had thought to drop the tree and his horse had quieted a bit, an Indian brave was there.

"Peace, we have peace!" the red man cried, holding out the pipe.

Joe grabbed the thing—what it was he didn't know. He stuck it in his mouth. There was no other way of holding it, for he had all he could to stay in the saddle. The horse was wheeling; he was tired of his jaunt. He'd had his run and his mind was set for home. He turned himself around and set off at a trot.

By the time he got back to the store, where the men were still gathered, the horse had gentled down considerable. Joe could hardly believe he had got back without having his neck broken. He took the pipe from his mouth and held it out to see what it was the Indian fellow had offered him.

The men on the porch of the store let out a whoop. "They're routed!" they shouted and began to thump each other on the back. "The Indians have sent the peace pipe!"

"T-t-tore their camp all to pieces," stuttered Joe. He sank down on the steps, nearly finished off.

Old Joe had done it again. All by his lonesome he had met and routed the Indians—all two hundred of them. It was almost beyond belief. The men got on their horses and rode over to the camp to see for themselves.

Yes, it was true. There was the camp with nary an Indian to be seen. Marks of the horse's hoofs were everywhere. The wreckage of the teepees was mingled with broken pottery. Even the campfires were scattered though the coals were still hot.

Well, there never was a man like Joe, the settlers all decided then and there.

"He ought to be commander of the state militia," said the miller. "He ought to have the job of defending the whole state."

"It's the kind of job he's fitten for!" the others heartily agreed.

When they got back to the store, they put it up to Joe. "You're the man for the job," they told him, "the job of defending the state from whatsoever and whosoever should attack it."

"No, boys." Joe shook his head. "I'm getting old. I've done enough. I hereby resign from public life. I don't even want to be sheriff any more. I want to settle down on my farm and live a quiet life. Don't call on me for anything else. I'm through."

That was his say and he stuck to it.

Well, in the end, the men had another meeting in the store. They decided that sure enough Joe had done his part for the settlement. He'd earned his rest. Out of gratitude for his defeat of the Indians, they voted him a pension, a nice tidy sum to be paid him every month for the rest of his life.

So, at last, Joe and Tildy were able to settle down and live peacefully on their little farm.

Surprise for the Black Bull

It was right after breakfast. Ma Cullifer stood in her bare feet in the muddy road and called out to the two children on the porch of the small log shanty.

"I'll be back before nightfall if nothing happens. If you get through the work early you can go out and play under the cypress tree."

The faces of Bess and Joe lit up. There was a vine looped among the high branches of the cypress tree. With a running leap they could grasp it and swing into the air far out over the cornfield.

"Yes, Ma," Bess and Joe called out. "We'll get along all right."

Ma waved good-by and strode off down the road. Her stout rawhide shoes hung around her neck by their laces. No use to ruin them in all this mud. Time enough to put them on just before she got there. Her basket of curing herbs was on her arm. Mistress Mason had sent word earlier that her baby was sick and to come right away.

The children would be all right. Bess was twelve years old. She could get the churning done and put the turnip greens and meat into the pot for dinner. And ten-year-old Joe had the onion patch to hoe; that would keep him out of mischief.

The bears and wildcats never ventured out of the woods in the daytime any more and Ma would be back before nightfall.

And then, all of a sudden, Ma stopped short in the road. She'd forgotten to warn the children about the tax collector!

Two times a year everybody in the new colony of North Carolina had to pay his share of the money to carry on the government. By rights, it shouldn't be much. It never had been until lately. But now the Governor had started to build a fine palace for himself at the capital in New Bern and he was squeezing the money for it out of poor settlers like themselves. If they didn't have money then the tax collector seized whatever they did have. Only a month ago the man had taken Mistress Mundy's good homespun dress, and before that he seized a neighbor's horse. Suppose he came while she was away and took their cow, Flossie! There would be no more butter and no milk for the children. And the black bull! If he should get the black bull whatever would they do? When folks didn't own a horse or mule to do their plowing, a bull did well enough. He pulled the plow, hauled logs out of the field after they were cut down, and dragged the corn to the mill on the wooden sled. They would be ruined without the black bull. They could not plant their crops and make a living.

For a minute, Ma thought of going back. Then she looked down at the basket of curing herbs. Suppose the baby died without her? That would be worse. No, she'd go on, she decided.

Back at the cabin, Bess and Joe hurried through the tasks Ma had set them. Bess churned the butter and paddled it into a round yellow ball, while Joe worked in the onion patch. Then they cut some turnip greens for dinner, pulled some of the new corn for roasting, and gathered some butter beans.

While they were preparing the vegetables for the pot, a man

rode up on a handsome white horse. Bess and Joe were so impressed with his fine flaring coat, polished boots, cocked hat, and fancy vest that they hardly had presence of mind to bob and curtsey when he spoke to them.

The man dismounted, tied his horse to the limb of a mulberry tree, and inquired where their parents were.

"Pa's gone turkey-hunting and Ma's at Mistress Mason's house tending her sick baby," Bess informed him.

"Well, now, it's too bad they're not here, for I was hoping they might have a bite to eat to offer a weary traveler," the stranger said.

"Dinner will soon be done if you've a mind to wait for it," Bess answered.

She knew that Ma would want her to offer hospitality to any who came along the road. There were few inns in this wild country and the houses were many miles apart.

The stranger thanked her, drank a gourd full of fresh water

that Joe brought from the well, then sat down on the porch to smoke his pipe while he waited for dinner. Joe, awed by the newcomer, sat down on the edge of the porch, but could not think of anything to say.

At last the stranger spoke. "That's a fine-looking cow you have out there at the barn. Is she yours?"

"Yes, she's ours and her name is Flossie. We've got a black bull, too. There he is out under the tree. We've got some hogs, two hogs, nice and fat. We're pretty well off, I reckon." Joe wanted to impress the stranger with their importance.

"Got lots of money on hand?" the man inquired.

'Well, no sir. Pa says there's no money circulating. Only sometimes some Spanish gold pieces and now and then some English silver, but we don't ever see any of that. But we've got plenty without money. Bess has a new homespun dress in the chest, dyed with indigo, and I've got a buckskin shirt trimmed with squirrel skins. Maybe come winter we'll have some shoes—maybe some boots like yours," Joe boasted a little.

"Uh-huh! Well, you *are* well fixed." The stranger nodded with satisfaction.

Inside the cabin, Bess was bustling about. She laid the trencher table with wooden plates and a spoon for each.

As soon as the food was done, Bess poured buttermilk from the churn into the earthenware pitcher. Then she called out that dinner was ready.

The gentleman sat down, took a neat little case from his pocket that contained a folding knife and fork, opened them, and ate in a manner so elegant that the children were more impressed with him than ever.

After a hearty meal he sat back from the table and said, "I'm sorry your father is away, children. I'm the tax collector and I must take what is owed. Your father is behind with his payments. If you've any money in the house, you'd better let me have it."

Bess and Joe were speechless. Well they knew about the tax collector. But they had pictured him as some sort of a monster, not as a rich and handsome gentleman.

"We've no money, sir," Bess stammered at last.

"Then I'll have to take the cow."

"Oh, sir, we couldn't get along without the cow. We'd have no milk or butter!"

"Oh well, then, the black bull will do. Fetch him from the barn," the man said.

Bess and Joe looked at each other. Both understood what the black bull meant to them. If only they had suspected that the stranger was the tax collector, they might have got all the stock hidden back in the deep woods. Bess began to think quickly.

"If the bull must go, he'd better have a good meal before-hand," she said. "And, sir, I wouldn't like for you to leave without a snack to take along. If you'll wait on the porch I'll fix you some ham and corn pone, and Joe can run out to the barn and feed the animals."

The collector looked distrustful. He would go with Joe to the barn, he said. Bess hurried about getting the food ready for the animals while Joe and the collector waited on the porch.

"Here's the swill for the hogs." Bess handed Joe the wooden bucket. Gathering up an armful of shucks from the corn that had been cooked that day, she thrust them into a basket.

"Be sure to give these to the black bull and some to the cow," she admonished Joe.

Joe and the collector walked out to the barn. First Joe poured out the swill into the hog trough, then he hurried to the barn and emptied the basket of shucks for the cattle.

They were on their way back to the house when a strange and frightful racket broke out in the pigpen. Joe and the collector looked back.

The two hogs were jumping about like crazy things, squealing frantically. One after the other, they leaped the fence and ran madly toward the woods.

Hardly had they disappeared when the bull let out a roar, threw up his tail, crashed through the fence, and tore off to the woods. After him ran the cow, mooing insanely.

While Joe and the collector stood staring, the collector's horse began to act up like the other animals. Rearing and plunging, he pulled away from the mulberry limb and galloped off down the road.

"Whoa there, whoa!" With a yell, the collector ran after his horse. It would never do to be left afoot in this trackless wilderness, and New Bern all of fifty miles away! It was the last the children saw of him.

In the late afternoon Ma returned. The first thing she saw was the hoofprints of the horse under the mulberry tree. The children were sitting, giggling, on the porch.

"Who's been here?" Ma cried out.

"The tax collector!" replied Bess and Joe in one breath.

"But he didn't get anything!" Joe cried hastily. "No, not a thing! First he said he would take the cow and then he said he would take the bull, but Bess took care of him, all right. He went off a-running!"

"I'm sorry, Ma, but we haven't any more red peppers," said Bess soberly. "I put half of them in the hogs' bucket and the other half in with the shucks for the cattle. It must have burnt them up. They broke down the fences and went running off to the woods!"

"But the collector—" gasped Ma. "He went off without taking *anything*?"

"His horse ran off," giggled Bess. "I put a pine burr under his tail. And the collector took off after him."

"Young'uns!" exclaimed Ma, sinking into a chair, "you've saved us, sure enough. I couldn't have done as well myself!"

The Voice in the Jug

There was once a man and his wife who lived off yonder in the mountains. Their names were Dade and Minnie. All they had in the world was a log cabin Dade had built himself, a cornfield planted on a steep mountainside, a brindled cow, a Dominicker hen, and a rangy razorback sow. But somehow, with the corn they raised, the milk and butter from the cow, the eggs from the hen, and now and then a litter of pigs from the sow, they got along.

Then one year they had a run of bad luck. A cloudburst sent such a torrent of water rushing down the mountain that it carried Dade's cornfield clean away, a fox stole the Dominicker hen, and the brindled cow slipped and fell over the edge of a cliff. That left only the razorback sow to ward off starvation.

"I reckon we'll have to sell her to buy food," said Dade. "With nary a dust of meal to make corn bread, no milk, butter or eggs, how can we live?"

It made Minnie sad to think of parting with the sow, but there was nothing to do but give her consent. So one morning, just at sunup, Dade put off down the mountain with the sow following along on the end of a rope. He aimed to lead her down to the town, a day's trip away, where he could get the best price for her.

Not far from home he came to a shallow creek bubbling along over the stones and he sat down and took off his shoes and began wading along it. It was the quickest and easiest way down from the mountains. As he was spattering along with the sow at his heels, feeling very downcast, he noticed a jug bobbing along in the stream.

At first he thought he would pick it out of the water and take it along with him. If it was a good jug, it would come in handy sometime or other. But then he said to himself, "It's only something worthless or it wouldn't have been thrown away. I shan't burden myself with it." And he waded on past it down the stream.

Then to his surprise, he heard a voice. "Hey, you!" It was a spiteful, twanging, shut-up voice.

Dade stopped a moment. It might have been only the shrilling of a cricket.

"Hey, you, come back and let me out of here!" The words seemed to come from the floating jug. "If you know what's good for you, you'll let me out in a hurry!"

Dade stood perplexed while the jug floated nearer, then he reached down and lifted it from the water. It was a good solid earthenware jug, all in one piece and tightly stoppered.

"Come on now. Don't waste time—pull out the stopper!" commanded the voice. It did indeed come from inside the jug.

Dade was flabbergasted. He stood holding the jug, hardly believing his ears.

"Don't stand there like a goof," the voice came spanging sharply. "Open the cork now and let me out!"

Now Dade was a canny mountain man. He hadn't been born yesterday. A voice corked up in a jug was a mighty curious thing. Who knows what might come pouring out if he pulled the cork! He stood fingering it, studying what to do.

"I can see you're a kind, goodhearted man," the voice took on a wheedling tone. "It's mighty cramped quarters in here and I'm a-suffering something terrible. I've a crick in my neck and both feet have gone to sleep. If you'd only take the trouble to pull out the cork it would be a deed of kindness."

"Who—who might you be in there?" stammered Dade.

"If you want to know the truth, I'm the old Boogerman, that's who I am. Now let me out! I've a deal of business that's been neglected."

Dade gave a start and almost dropped the jug. The old Devil himself! "Excuse me, sir," he recovered enough to ask, "but what might you be doing shut up in a jug?"

"As you might know, it was a woman that got me into it!"

"Must of been a powerful strong woman to cram the Devil into a jug," said Dade.

"No, it wasn't," the voice rasped sullenly. "It was a little bitty body as frail as a dandelion. You'd never think she had it in her to do such a trick. But here I am corked up like a blackberry cordial and not able to stir hand nor foot."

"If you're the old Boogerman"—there was a doubting sound in Dade's voice— "you ought to be able to push out the cork yourself. Can't you do witchcraft and magic and all like that?"

"Haven't you seen what's on the cork?" snapped the voice.

Dade looked down and examined the cork. A cross was painted on the top of it.

"There—you see! That's the one sign the Devil can't pass. Oh, that little gal knew what she was about. She was a smart one, she was!"

"How did she manage to get you in there?" Dade was full of curiosity.

"Let me out first and I'll tell you all about it."

"Oh, no," replied Dade craftily. "Tell me first and then I'll consider what to do."

"Seeing as how you've got me at a disadvantage, I might as well tell you," buzzed the old Boogerman inside the jug. "You'll see, all right, how badly I was mistreated. Well, as you know, I pass through the mountains now and again. Oh, you wouldn't recognize me for the Devil if you met me on the road. I can take any shape and mostly I walk around looking like any other man, only a mite handsomer and a sight more friendly. It's easier to make trouble if you're handsome and have a smooth tongue."

"But—but the jug here," Dade reminded him. "You were going to tell me how the woman put you into the jug."

"I'm a-coming to it in time," said the voice impatiently. "You see, there's an old granny-woman up the mountain a piece. She's somewhat of a witch. Sometimes she calls on me to help turn a body's cow sick or to throw a misery onto someone she's got a spite against. Well, one day I was there stirring up a brew for her, when outen the house floated this pretty little gal. She was golden-haired and light as a dandelion in a mountain breeze. You'd never believe a pretty little thing like that could belong to such an old hag; but sure enough, she was the old woman's daughter.

"I put on my handsomest looks and my best smile," buzzed the voice. "And I made up to that little gal like anything. I courted her day in and day out, and finally she agreed to marry me. The old granny-woman wasn't so pleased at the idea of her daughter marrying the Devil, but I figured she would be afraid to say anything. Anyway, one day the gal and I went a-horseback down to Judge Canton's house at the county seat and we got us spliced.

"Oh, I was a happy bridegroom, I can tell you. The gal looked happy, too. And that shows how deceitful she was. When we got back to her cabin she led me into a little back room and closed the door. She locked this door and put the key in her pocket.

"I took one look around the room and let out a yell. I knew I'd been betrayed and I knew I'd have to get out of that room right away or I'd wither up like an old dried leaf."

"Whatever was the matter?" asked Dade.

"There were signs of the cross everywhere I looked," moaned the voice. "Even knives and forks were crossed on the table. I turned to the gal. Was she the one who had tricked me or was it her old hag of a mother? There she stood laughing in my face.

" 'Oh, you thought you had me fooled,' she said. 'You thought I didn't know who you were, Mr. Devil. But I knew all the time and now I've got you. I reckon you won't go traipsing around fooling any more women.'

"That made me boiling mad." The shut-up voice buzzed like a wasp. "I turned myself into a flash of lightning. I meant to blast that gal to a cinder, but when I looked she'd streaked the sign of the cross on her forehead with some soot from the chimney. I couldn't touch her. And I felt myself wilting. I had to get out of there. Up the chimney, of course! But there in front of it was a cross marked on the hearth and another was in the back of the chimney. I couldn't escape that way. The windows were marked, too. I looked around for any chink or cranny. There wasn't a one.

"Then my eyes lit on the keyhole. I laughed aloud. It wasn't marked. They'd forgotten it. Or so I thought. I turned myself into a puff of smoke and began to stream through it.

"But I hadn't given enough credit to that old granny-witch. She was outside the door holding this here jug to the keyhole. Before I knew what had happened I found myself inside it. The old hag popped the cork in and there I was."

"My, my!" Dade shook his head. "You never can tell what women will think up."

"You sure can't," the Boogerman agreed. "The two of 'em, mother and daughter, went to laughing fit to kill. They took the jug up the side of the mountain and buried it in the ground."

"In the ground!" exclaimed Dade in surprise. "Then how did you happen to be in the creek?"

"It was that cloudburst a few days ago. All that water pouring down the slopes unearthed the jug and washed it into the creek. You see now what a mean trick those women played on me? Come on, now. We men have to stick together. Be a good fellow and let me out."

Dade turned the jug round and round in his hands. It occurred to him that a talking jug might be a very profitable possession.

"I'll think it over," he said evasively.

"What's there to think over?"

Dade didn't answer. He put the jug under his arm, gave the

sow's rope a twitch, and off he went sloshing along the creek. Inside the jug the voice buzzed and whanged and zinged like a hive of angry bees, but Dade ignored it. He'd got a fine idea and he meant to carry it out. "When I get down to town, I'll get me some old empty crates and I'll build me a little booth like they have for side shows at the county fair," he said to himself. "Then I'll charge money for people to come in and hear the talking jug."

When he reached the town it did not take Dade long to carry out his plans. In no time he had a little booth set up with the jug inside. The town square was crowded. Men stood around, trading horses or selling sheep or cattle. The women had set out jams and jellies they hoped to sell, or had hung up patch-work quilts and hooked rugs. Vendors walked around with splint-bottom chairs they'd made from stout hickory limbs and baskets woven from rushes. Others peddled pillows stuffed with goose feathers, and good strong pottery ware. Oh, there was a parcel of people on hand! At first no one paid any attention when Dade began to shout that he had a talking jug. Then a few people strolled over, paid the quarter to buy a ticket, and walked into the booth.

When they came out again their eyes were bugged out like marbles. The old Boogerman had put on a performance for sure. Oh, he was mad a sight. He'd yelled and threatened in that twanging, shut-up voice of his, he'd bawled and bellowed and shrieked out all the bad words he could think of. Everybody who'd heard him came out petrified with astonishment. It didn't take them long to spread the word around.

In no time, such a crowd was clamoring to get into Dade's booth that he couldn't take in the money fast enough.

The upshot of it was that he arrived home that night with a tow sack full of coins and bills and the sow still following on the end of the rope. When Minnie saw her husband unloading all that money she was terror-struck. She thought he'd lost his senses and robbed a bank. But no, Dade assured her, he'd made it all in an honest way. And he explained to her what had happened.

After that, there was nary a soul from one end of the mountains to the other as joyful as Minnie.

Dade was full of plans for making money with the Devil in the jug. The next day he set off for the county fair where he set up a booth on the midway. After that it was court week in the county seat. People that had fallen afoul of the law were glad to take their minds off their troubles by a look at the now famous talking jug. Oh, there was always an affair of one sort or another down in the valley and Dade was sure to be there with his booth and his talking jug.

Up at the cabin in the mountains, he and Minnie had money and to spare. They bought several cows. They cleared some new land for a cornfield and bought a mule for plowing it. There was new furniture for the house, some fine dresses for Minnie and some good suits for Dade. Oh, things were going fine for them!

And then one day Dade went off to buy a piece of land he'd set his heart on. He left the jug sitting on the mantelpiece, with a word of caution to Minnie. She was to make sure that nothing jostled it or caused it to fall. She was to watch out and see that nothing happened to it.

"I'll take the best of care of it, don't worry!" Minnie promised. She sat down and began to churn the rich cream from the fine milk the new cows gave. Her husband had not been gone long when derisive laughter began to sound from the jug.

"Ha, ha, ha!"

"What are you laughing at?" asked Minnie uneasily, for she could never feel quite right about having the old Boogerman in the house.

"I'm laughing at that husband of yours," the voice rasped. "He's a dunderhead if I ever saw one!"

"What's he done to make you call him a dunderhead?" Of course, Minne knew well enough that Dade *was* a dunderhead, in spite of the fact that he'd been making so much money lately. Hadn't he planted his cornfield where the water could wash it away, and hadn't he let the cow fall off the cliff? She didn't think of the time she, herself, had left the hen house unlocked for the fox to steal the hen.

"I've offered him a chance to make big money," buzzed the voice. "I'm laughing to think what an idiot he is not to take it. Why, you could be sitting in a big white house like Judge Canton's down at the county seat and riding around in a fine automobile if your husband had the sense he was born with. But no, he must go traipsing from one poor little gathering to the next, making a few measly pennies."

Minnie was taken aback. The money brought home by her husband seemed to her nothing short of a fortune. "But—but —how could he do better?" she stammered.

"Don't you know that all the money in the world is at my command? I've only to say the word and you'd see your table there piled up with greenbacks as high as the cciling."

It was true, of course. The Devil had worldly power. Minnie did not doubt it for one moment. It came to her that maybe she could manage better than her husband. "What could we do to be rich?" she inquired.

"Only a small thing. I want the stopper taken out of the jug. Pull it out and I promise you I'll leave your table piled up with so much money you'll never be able to spend it all."

"Shucks," said Minnie craftily. "It's easy to promise. How do I know you wouldn't fly out and forget all about your promise? Oh, I'd have to see the money before I opened the jug."

Instantly the table gave a loud creak. It was suddenly loaded with packages of money that reached clean up to the rafters. Minnie's eyes popped open. She could hardly get her breath for looking at the huge mound of bills.

"It's all yours, if you pull out this cork," the Boogerman whispered as softly as the sighing of the wind. "If you don't let me go," he suddenly snapped, "I'll take it away and you'll never get the chance again."

There it was in plain sight. Minnie put her hand on it. Yes, it was real. There was no shamming or monkey business about it. She stumbled to the mantel, took down the jug, and pulled out the cork.

Instantly, there was a terrific flash of lightning. The logs of the cabin flew apart like straws. The money on the table burst into flame. It burned up in a moment. And the thunder-clap that followed frightened all the livestock so that the cows and the mule ran mooing and braying over the cliff. The Boogerman's laughter went rolling across the sky.

That night when Dade came home he found Minnie lying stunned among the ruins. He fetched some water from the spring and brought her to. She gasped out the story of what had happened. They got up and began to look over their possessions. Nothing was left except their old friend, the razor-back sow.

"I reckon we'll have to sell her," Dade said.

There was nothing for Minnie but to give her consent. So off went Dade as sad as could be with the sow on the end of the rope. Down the stream he went, thinking how useless it was to make any bargain with the Devil. When he came to the place where he had found the jug, he looked and looked again. But there was no jug there and he never found another like it.

The Goat That Went
to School

When the clouds hung heavy about the mountains, Hubert could step outside the cabin and wash his face in their damp white mist. That was how high up he lived. His pappy's little log house was built on the steep side of old Thunderhead Mountain, so far up that the valley down below looked misty blue like an opal. The houses down there in the settlement seemed tinier than matchboxes. It was easy to pick out the schoolhouse from the others for its new tin roof glittered in the sun and sent up shafts of light like a diamond.

Hubert sat on a rock ledge in front of his home and stared down at the bright roof longingly. He was ten years old and he had never been to school.

Around by the road it was a far piece to the school in the valley. It took a whole day to get there. But Hubert knew a short cut. Though it was a steep and toilsome way, zigzagging down the face of the mountain, Hubert could make it in an hour.

But when he pleaded with his mother to let him go down and get some learning, she always said, "I'm afeard for you to walk it alone in the wintertime. If the snow began to fly, pretty soon the trail would be covered as smooth and as white as a fresh-made feather bed, and you'd not know which-a-way to turn. You'd go wandering on the mountains until you were lost and frozen with the cold. No, you'll have to make out for a while longer with what your pappy and I can teach you."

But Hubert didn't forget about the school. All the boys down in the valley went there. They learned how to read stories out of books, tales of cowboys and hunts and other things that boys like to read of. And they played games down there in the valley, fox-in-the-war and baseball; and at the end of the year they had a "speaking" and each pupil would go up and say a little piece, all dressed in his Sunday best. It was something to wish for!

"Can't I just *start* this year, Mammy," begged Hubert, "and go until the days begin to get cold and it looks like snow?"

"Well, I suppose there'd be no harm in that," said his mammy. "You can go during the month of September. There's never any snow in September." Hubert was joyful. Even one month in school was something to look forward to.

Now Hubert began to worry about his clothes. All he had to wear was a pair of blue overalls and a homespun shirt. The other boys in the school would have on short, store-bought pants and nice striped shirts. And then there were books. Where would he get the money for books?

There was always plenty to eat in the little cabin on Thunderhead Mountain, for Pappy raised everything they needed. There were warm clothes, too, for Mammy spun the wool from their own sheep and wove it into cloth. But there was never any money to spare, and Hubert did want some clothes like the other boys had and some books so that he could study his lessons.

If there were only a way he could earn a little money! Hubert cudgeled his brains. One day he said to his mammy, "I think I'll go ask Mr. Honeycutt if he would like some help picking his apples and loading 'em into the wagon to take to town. Maybe I could make me a little money to buy some store clothes and some books."

"Go right ahead," his mammy nodded. "Asking won't hurt."

Hubert set off, plodding around the mountain to his neighbor's farm in the next cove.

"Why, yes, I can use a little help loading my apples," said Mr. Honeycutt, twisting his handle-bar mustaches.

Hubert set to work picking up the sound apples from the ground, plucking the ripe ones from the tree, sacking them, and helping Mr. Honeycutt to hoist them into his covered wagon. When it was loaded high, Mr. Honeycutt hitched his old brown mule between the shafts, then he climbed into the driver's seat.

"I'll not forget you when I sell my apples in the town," he promised as he cracked his whip and went creaking down the rough mountain road. "I'll be back in two or three days and I'll stop by your house with your pay."

During the time Mr. Honeycutt was away, Hubert wondered if he would get a good price for his apples. He hoped so, for if he did, he might pay enough for picking them so Hubert could buy all the things he wanted.

"If he pays me only enough to get part of them," he thought, "I'll buy me the store-bought pants first." A homespun shirt wouldn't look so outlandish if he had a pair of proper pants to go with it. After that he would buy a reader.

On the third day when he heard the rumble of Mr. Honeycutt's wagon wheels coming around the mountain, he ran to the cabin door.

"Whoa!" cried Mr. Honeycutt, pulling up in front of the door. "Well, Hubert, I've got your pay!" He was smiling so that his handle-bar mustaches spread out over his face.

He must have got a good price, and he's going to pay me a lot, thought Hubert, taking note of his good humor. He ran out to the covered wagon and looked up expectantly.

Mr. Honeycutt leaned into the back of the wagon behind the white canvas top and began to pull something forward. "Well, here's your pay. How do you like it?"

Around the edge of the wagon top peeped a neat, fur-covered head with two dainty horns. A goat! A trim little brown beard wiggled merrily as his jaws worked. The goat was chewing busily on the end of something white. It was Mr. Honeycutt's shirttail.

"Here! How did you get a-holt of that?" Mr. Honeycutt cried, pulling it away from his passenger and stuffing the ragged edge back into the top of his trousers.

"Well, how do you like him?" he asked, turning back to Hubert. "He cost a little more than I ought to pay for having my apples picked, but then I remembered how a boy loves a goat."

Hubert was surprised but it would not do to let Mr. Honeycutt see that he was disappointed to get a goat instead of money. Besides, it was a pretty, neat-looking little goat and he had always wanted one.

"Gee, Mr. Honeycutt, he sure is a fine goat. I thank you, I sure do!" He took the goat's rope and the trim little animal bounded gracefully out of the wagon.

"Land sakes! What have you got there?" asked Mammy when she saw the goat stepping along into the house beside Hubert.

"Well, I've got me a goat, though it's not what I expected. It's my pay for picking Mr. Honeycutt's apples."

"But I thought you wanted some money to get yourself some clothes to wear to school, and maybe some books."

"It's what he brought me," said Hubert, "and I'd as soon have him."

The goat made himself right at home. Hubert fixed him a nice bed of leaves in a corner of the woodshed and he fed him some corn or oats every day and let him crop the grass in front of the cabin.

The goat was never too busy eating to stop for a tussle with Hubert, for he was frisky and full of fun. He would rear up on his hind legs and butt at Hubert playfully and sometimes, when Hubert bent over to pick up something, he ran at him from behind and sent him tumbling.

One time he did it when Hubert was pouring a bucket full of buttermilk for the pigs. Over Hubert went, sprawling into the trough full of buttermilk. He went squishing and squashing to the house with streams of buttermilk running from his clothes, from his hair, and even from his ears.

When she saw the mischief the goat had done, his mammy said, "That goat's going to be a nuisance. You had as well take him down to town and sell him. Then you'd have the money to buy your things."

Hubert shook his head. Naughty as the goat was, he had learned to love him. He didn't like to think of selling him, even for some new clothes and his books. There must be another way of making a little money.

One day he had a bright idea. "I think I'll go along to Mr. Posey's place and see if he needs some help with his molasses."

"It won't hurt to ask," said Mammy. And so off Hubert went. He was hardly out of his own yard when he heard a scampering of small feet and the goat ran alongside. Hubert was pleased to have his company and soon they arrived at the Poseys' cabin.

"Well now, I might need someone to help me," said Mr. Posey, rubbing his bald head. "It's a lot of work making molasses, cutting the sugar cane in the fields, driving the mule around and around to squeeze the juice in the homemade molasses mill, then standing over the juice and boiling and boiling it until it gets thick and sweet and heavy. I've already made one big barrel full. It was a sight of trouble, but if I do say so, it's pretty good molasses. Would you like a taste?"

"Yes, sir," Hubert nodded. The old man leaned over and dipped into the barrel with a large spoon.

It was a nice invitation to the goat. He stood off a little way, then came at Mr. Posey with a rush. He sent him sprawling headfirst into the barrel of molasses.

Mr. Posey floundered out looking like a tar baby, covered from head to foot with thick black molasses.

"Get along!" he sputtered, wiping the molasses out of his face. "Get along home with that mischievous goat!"

Sorrowfully Hubert walked along home, and the goat went mincing along beside him.

"Just see what you've done," he said. "But for you, I'd have had a chance to make me a little money."

"Baa, baa, baa!" said the goat, as cheerfully as though he had not just butted his master out of a good job.

"Just as I told you, you had better take him down to the town and sell him," urged Mammy when she heard of the mischief the goat had done. "He'll never be anything but a nuisance. Then you could buy your things."

But Hubert did not care to part with his goat. "He'll not be naughty again," he said. "I'll try him a while longer."

The next day he went about his chores with a thoughtful face. He was trying hard to think of another way to earn some money. After a while he had a bright idea. "I think I'll go a-berrying," he said to his mammy. "Maybe I can pick enough to sell in the town and then I could buy my things."

"It's worth trying," said Mammy.

Before he left to go a-berrying, Hubert took a stout piece of rope and tied the goat to a tree. "You're a troublemaker," he said, "and you'd best stay here where you'll be out of mischief."

Off he started with a big basket over his arm. He was only halfway to the peak where the biggest blackberries grew when he heard a noise behind him. He turned and looked and there was the goat tripping daintily up the steep stony trail, dragging his rope all frayed and chewed.

"How did you get loose?" cried Hubert, but just the same he was half glad to see his friend. All day long he picked berries on the high mountainside and the goat was as good as could be. When his basket was full, Hubert set off for home.

"Mammy, Mammy, come and see!" he cried when he got

there. "Come and see how many berries I've got. And they're nice ones. I'll get a good price for them." He set his basket on the edge of the porch and ran to find Mammy.

When he got back, he found the basket tipped over. His berries were spilled on the ground and all scuffed and crushed. The goat's mouth was stained with blackberry juice.

"I told you so," cried Mammy, when she saw the mischief. "That goat is nothing but a nuisance. Why don't you take him down to the town and sell him?"

Hubert looked at his naughty goat regretfully. Perhaps he should take Mammy's advice. He'd likely get enough money for the goat to buy everything he needed, even a green-striped shirt and books. But the more he thought about it, the more he hated to part with his pet.

"I think I'll give him another chance," he decided.

For a while the goat would go along as good as yellow gold. But as surely as Hubert would think up a way to make a little money, he would break out with a piece of naughtiness and spoil all Hubert's chances.

That was the reason that on the first day of September Hubert set off sadly for the school, wearing the same old homespun shirt and his old blue overalls. He left the goat at home shut up tight in the woodshed. But not quite tight enough, for when he was only about halfway down the mountain he heard a quick trip-tripping behind him. He looked around and there was the goat prancing merrily after him.

Hubert frowned at him. "If it hadn't been for you I would have been going to school with some new store-bought pants and a nice striped shirt," he said, "and I would have had some books to study from."

"Baa, baa, baa!" bleated the goat as gaily as though his master were dressed in brand-new clothes. Down, down, down, they wound until at last they came to the school.

"Oh, look!" cried the children. "A new boy! And he has a goat!" They crowded around Hubert. No one noticed his faded shirt and his old blue overalls for they were much too busy asking questions about the goat.

The goat pranced with delight at seeing so many children. He stood up on his hind legs and butted the boys. He chased the girls. Then he let each one ride on his back. Everyone wanted to be friends with Hubert and his goat.

When the school bell rang, the goat lay down on the porch and waited while the children marched in for their lessons. Hubert went uneasily. What shall I do for books? he thought. But as soon as he was seated the teacher handed him a pile of them. There was an arithmetic, a speller, and a reader.

"They're yours for the year," she smiled at him. "The State furnishes all our books. You're only supposed to keep them nice and clean so that next year another boy can use them."

Every day during the month of September when the leaves were turning red and gold and brown on the shaggy mountain-sides, Hubert wound happily down the trail to the schoolhouse with the goat beside him. He did not mind the long hard trip, and neither did the goat. Hubert studied his lessons hard for he knew that pretty soon cold weather would come and the danger of snow. He wanted to learn as much as he could.

If only he could keep on going. Perhaps if he put his mind to it, he could think up a way. But think as he would, not an idea came.

Then came the end of September. It was his last day in school. Hubert told his friends good-by and started sadly for home.

As he climbed slowly up the mountain he noticed that the sky was dark and leaden. He was hardly halfway home when soft feathery flakes began to float downward among the tree trunks. Snow in September! It couldn't be! As the white flakes flew thicker and thicker, Hubert hurried his footsteps. He remembered what his mother had said about getting lost.

'Baa, baa, baa!" bleated the goat as happily as though the whirling flakes were not fast covering up the ground, hiding the trail, making everything look strange. Hubert stopped and looked all around. His eyes were wide and frightened.

Everything looked white and cold and unfamiliar. He couldn't tell which way to go. Any way he turned might start him rambling and he would be lost—lost in a snowstorm on Thunderhead Mountain.

But the goat seemed not to have a worry in his head. He frolicked ahead, bleating at Hubert, "Baa, baa, baa!" Now and then, he returned to nip at his trouser-legs. It was as though he were saying, "Come on, what are you waiting for?" It gave Hubert a glint of hope.

Perhaps he knows the way, Hubert thought. He put his hand on the smooth back and stumbled along where the goat led. They climbed and climbed. With his eyes half-closed to keep the snow from blinding him, Hubert did not know where he was going. But the goat stepped confidently as though he were sure of the ground and at last Hubert felt himself on a level place.

Could it be that they had reached the clearing where the cabin was? Hubert's heart gave a leap. He shielded his eyes with his hands and peered about. Dimly through the falling snow he could make out a building straight ahead. It was—yes, it was the cabin! He broke into a run.

When he pushed open the door, his mother started up. She cried joyfully, "Hubert!" She hugged him tight. "Your pappy was just setting off to look for you! I was afeard you were lost in the snow!"

"Not with a goat like this!" cried Hubert, flinging the door wide so that his pet could come in and warm himself beside the hearth fire. "I couldn't tell which-a-way or where to turn, but he stepped right out and led me straight along home!"

"If that goat could lead you through a storm like this," spoke up Pappy, "he could lead you through anything. And you never need fear getting lost between here and the schoolhouse."

"I reckon you're right," agreed Mammy.

After that there was nothing to keep Hubert from going to school during the rest of the year.

Every day through the fall, the winter, and the spring, he and his goat zigzagged down the mountain trail together. Hubert learned to write and to figure sums and to read. But for all the time the goat spent in school, the only thing he ever learned was how to chew tobacco.

However, the goat was never left out of anything, not even from the speakings on the last day of school. The children went into the woods that day and gathered armfuls of bright red mountain laurel and pale pink rhododendron. They plucked great bunches of shiny heart leaves and then made garlands to hang about the little stage at the end of the school room. When they were finished it looked beautiful.

The lamps were lighted that night. The mothers and fathers and all their kin were there to hear the children speak their pieces, and hardly anybody made a mistake. When his turn came, Hubert walked proudly out on the stage. But before he reached the center he heard a trip-trip-tripping. He turned and looked and there was the goat stepping along behind him.

"Go back where you belong," whispered Hubert, but the goat didn't care to go back. He stood quietly while Hubert recited his piece. Hubert finished without a mistake and all the people clapped.

"Hurray! Hurray for Hubert!" they shouted.

Hubert bowed politely as the teacher had taught him to, and marched from the stage, but the goat, spying the beautiful green garlands hanging on the wall, went over and took a nip. Finding them tasty, he braced himself, pulled them down from the wall, and stood in the bright light in the middle of the stage, chewing with gusto.

"Hurray! Hurray for the goat!" shouted all the people, laughing and clapping as the curtain went down.

Janey's Shoes

With a last burst of speed, the Calloway children ran pell-mell through the gate and up the little walk in front of the log cabin on the side of White Doe Mountain.

"Granny! Hey there, Granny!"

"Why, bless my soul, it's the children!" exclaimed the little old woman on the porch, peering at them with dim eyes. They crowded around her, exclaiming, telling about the trip from the low country.

"Oh! Granny, its' such a hard pull up this trail!" exclaimed Ellen. "Why on earth did anybody want to build a house up this high?"

"We left early this morning," interrupted Jody, "and it's taken us until almost night. The car just huffed and puffed when we got up into the mountains, and the engine boiled so that we had to get out and walk the rest of the way. We left Mummy and Daddy back a ways."

"That last piece of trail was the worst! Just look at my new shoes, Granny!" Little Mary held out a shiny patent leather pump. "I got them scratched on the rocks."

"The first time I came up that trail," said Granny, gazing off toward the distant ranges, "I didn't have any shoes. I came over the rocks barefoot in the snow."

"No shoes!" Ellen exclaimed, horror-struck. The others looked at the old lady in silent surprise.

"No shoes," stated Granny positively. "And it was a long time before I got any. Pa and Ma and I had been a-living down in South Carolina where the land is flat—just where you live now. We were poor. You children wouldn't be able to understand how poor we were. It was before the Civil War, and all around us were the great rich plantations with Negro slaves, thousands of them, working, raising cotton that went off by great shiploads to foreign countries.

"One day Ma and Pa hitched up the oxen to the oxcart and loaded everything we had onto it. Pa had made up his mind to move up into the mountains where the land was free, and where he wouldn't be looked down on and called poor white trash by any rich plantation owner.

"I would have to stay with a neighbor, they told me, till they got them a place and a house built; and they took me over to the neighbor's house and left me, along with all the clothes I had and a pair of shoes. Ma had made sure I had some shoes before she left me, because winter was not far off and she wanted to be certain I wouldn't have to go barefoot in the cold.

"Ma was a-crying when they left. I remember I felt the wet on her cheeks when she kissed me good-by. I hadn't thought much about it until then. But when I saw the oxcart disappear down the road with the cow following on behind, and everything I'd ever been used to piled in underneath the leather cover, I got a sharp hurting in my breast. But I didn't say anything and I didn't cry.

"The neighbor woman must have known how I felt though. She gave me a sugar rag to suck on."

"A sugar rag? What's that, Granny?" Mary asked.

"Why, in those days even a little taste of sugar was a treat to us. And the grown folks used to put a spoonful into a clean cloth and tie it up and let the children suck it so that it would last a long time. Well, anyway—" Granny continued her story, "I got along somehow, after they left, until night began to come on. Then I felt worse. I went to bed on a shuck mattress in a little room up under the eaves. The neighbor woman and her husband slept right next to me on another mattress. Everything seemed strange. The house creaked and outside, in the dark, little animals made scratching, tripping noises on the roof. I lay wide awake, listening and a-longing for Ma and Pa.

"After a while the man began to snore. I knew it wasn't anything to be afraid of, but somehow it was just the last straw that broke the camel's back. I rose up and felt around for my dress and slipped into it. Then I climbed down the ladder from the loft. On the way to the door I stumbled over a chair and made a great racket. The man stopped snoring and my heart started pumping like mad, but after a bit he started again. I tiptoed to the door and pulled the latchstring."

Granny's young listeners sat forward tensely. The old woman sat quiet for a moment, recalling the long ago. "It was a bright moonlight night," she went on. "I remember how pretty the road looked, shining and leading straight away to where Ma and Pa had gone. The dust felt cool to my bare feet and I started running. I ran and ran till I got out of breath and couldn't run any more. Then I walked. I'd come to crossroads now and then as I went along, but I never turned off. Seems like common sense told me to keep to the widest one. I walked all night long. I wasn't afraid, as you might think I would be out there on the road, alone at night, and me a little girl hardly eight years old. All I had in my mind was that I wanted to get with Ma and Pa.

"But just before the dawn a chill seemed to rise up out of the ground. I got cold and my spirits began to drop. It seemed

I'd never come up with my folks. I was so tired that I could hardly drag one foot after the other one, but somehow I kept a-going.

"Then up ahead, sort of standing out against the sunrise, I saw a woman in a black slat bonnet and a long dark dress like they used to wear in those days. She was leaning over, a-stirring a little flickering fire. I couldn't see her face but I knew in a flash who it was.

" 'Ma! Ma!' I flew to her and grabbed her around the knees and held her tight. Ma sat down on the ground and put her arms around me. I began to sob my heart out—all that I'd pent up the day before and all night on the road.

"Then Pa came up with an armful of wood for the fire. He just stood a-looking at me like he'd seen a ghost.

" 'What are we a-going to do with her, Pa?' Ma said, looking up at him. Seems like my heart choked into my mouth then; I looked up at him, too. Everything in the world for me seemed to hang on what he'd say. I just knew if he made me go back I'd never be able to face it.' "

The three children on the bench glanced at each other, dismay for that long-vanished little girl in their eyes. "Did—did he make you go back, Granny?" inquired Mary.

"We-e-ell, no," Granny said, smiling slowly. "He said to Ma, 'We'll fetch her along.'

" 'But she's got no clothes—except what's on her back! And her shoes! Where're your shoes, Janey?' Ma cried, shaking me by the shoulder. Shoes were hard for poor folks to get in those days. They were all made by hand out of leather that had taken a long time and a lot of trouble to tan. 'Where're your shoes?' Ma kept asking me.

"I never made any answer, but just kept sobbing. I'd had no thought of any shoes when I left. They'd been put away somewhere against the winter and, even if I'd thought of 'em, I'd not have known where to go looking for them.

" 'We'll fetch her along anyway,' Pa said shortly, and went over to the fire and laid the sticks on it.

"I never shall forget breakfast that morning," Granny's old face rippled into a beatific smile. "The sun was just a-coming up, edging everything with a little rim of gold, and the birds were a-twittering busily all around. I'd never known how nice it was just to be with my ma and pa. I sat on the ground between 'em, so close that I could reach out and touch either of 'em, and ate the hoecake and fried pork that Ma had cooked over the coals. And I tell you there never was and never will be anything that tasted any finer.

"As we were cleaning up after the breakfast, a fellow came by on horseback and Pa hailed him and asked him to tell the neighbor woman that I'd caught up with my folks in the night and that they were a-taking me on.

"When we started on again, they pulled back the leather wagon top and set me on a great big puffy feather bed high up on top of the load. It was as soft as a cloud and I just lay there, a-looking around at things and up at the sky and at Ma and Pa a-walking beside the cart and the two oxen plodding along, till the steady rocking of the cart and the creaking of the wheels fairly lulled me to sleep.

"Though we came the same way that you did today, it was a very different trip from yours. It took us a month to get to the foothills."

"A month, Granny!" exclaimed Jody in astonishment. "Just to come two hundred miles?"

"Why, yes, child, an ox travels slow. And the roads were bad. There were no fine highways such as you have today. Sometimes in rainy weather the cart wheels would sink down into the mud as far as the hub, and the poor oxen would pull and strain and not be able to move an inch. We'd have to wait until some other travelers came along to help get them out. Then sometimes we'd have to stop to pull other people's turn-outs from the mud.

"On we went that-a-way, day after day, with every day something different happening. Once I remember we met a drove of so many hogs that they halted us on the road and took a whole day to pass by."

The listening children made an exclamation of surprise.

"Why, yes," Granny said, "there were eight hundred of 'em, maybe a thousand, all moving at a snail's pace, walking along the road, with drivers on horseback on each side. Pa grumbled a sight and hollered at the drivers trying to make 'em open up a way for us, but the drivers said they couldn't do anything without stampeding their flock. In the end it was worth all the delay, for the next day we came upon a young sow lying beside the road. Her feet were all swollen and sore and she hadn't been able to keep up.

" 'Let's take her along,' Ma said.

" 'She's not rightly ours,' Pa said, 'but she'd only die here or be eaten up by some animal.'

"They had to do a lot of figuring and shifting about to get that hog onto the wagon, but they did it after a while. They emptied a big chest, and all the things that were in it they tied up in one of Ma's great wide petticoats, and they put that pig in the chest.

"Ma doctored her feet with turpentine. It was my job to keep her fed. We had brought barely enough food for the oxen and the cow and there wasn't any to spare for the sow. At night, when Ma was cooking supper, I'd dig for roots and bulbs and hunt around for wild fruits—just anything that the critter could eat. The poor thing kept getting thinner and thin-ner, no matter how I scratched around, but some way or other

I kept life in her and she lasted out the trip. She was a great blessing to me, too, as you'll find out, and well worth the bother.

"There was never any lack for something to see along the road. Several times we met fine carriages, a whole caravan of 'em at a time, each one full of fine ladies in silk and satin hoop skirts, chattering and laughing. There were black slaves along driving wagons full of brassbound trunks; and handsome young men on horseback riding along beside the carriages, talking to the ladies. They were planters' families, Pa said, who had come up from Charleston to spend the summer in the mountains away from the malaria and fevers of the lowlands.

"Once we met a long queue of Negro slaves chained together by their ankles, walking along all in step, singing a mournful sort of tune to the clanking of their chains. They belonged to a slave trader, Pa said, who was taking them down to Georgia to work in the sugar cane fields.

"Pa strode along the faster after that, like he was glad to be going the other way.

"When we passed through Saluda Gap in North Carolina and began to climb into the mountains proper, it just seemed to me that we were a-stepping up the stairs to heaven. Down below us we could see the country spread out, all blue and shimmery with the distance, and white clouds floating between us now and then. The mountains up ahead were as blue as sapphires and always a-changing color and a-shifting from one kind of blue to another.

"But the weather soon began to feel sharp, and I started to think of those shoes I'd left down there in the low country. My feet had got hard as hoofs with the walking, but they weren't used to the cold yet. I could sit on the load as long as we were going, with my feet folded under me, but when time came to make camp I'd have to get down and begin grubbing for the sow, no matter how cold it was. Ma and Pa had about all they could do to take care of the other animals and the cooking. I can tell you, many's the time I wished I'd taken thought to hunt around for those shoes before I left the neighbors' house that night!

"Well, at last we got to Asheville, away up in the hills. It was only a little village then with a few rough houses and muddy streets, but Pa thought it would be a good idea to get his land somewhere around—not too far away. He unhitched the oxen and left Ma and me for about a week while he went off to see about choosing a proper piece. When he got back he had a pleased look about him as though he'd found what he liked, and he hitched up the oxen and we started on right away.

"It was an unseasonable autumn that year. We'd hardly got going before it began to snow. I sat crouched under the wagon top wrapped up in an old red shawl, but Ma and Pa trudged outside just as usual till they looked like two snowbanks walking along.

"It was hard going for the oxen. The way was uphill and their feet kept slipping on the snow. By nightfall, when we got to that last steep stretch—the one you children were a-complaining of just now—the poor beasts were worn out. They struggled till they were wet with sweat, in spite of the cold weather, but they couldn't make it up that incline. After a while they stopped trying and just stood there panting.

" 'We can't push 'em past the breaking point,' Pa said. 'It's been a long hard trip for 'em and with shortened rations —I reckon they're plumb out of heart.' He took off their heavy wooden yokes and their harness and they lay down right where they were, in the snow. Pa covered 'em over with the leather cover from the wagon and said he'd just leave 'em there for the night.

" 'We'll have to go on afoot,' he said to Ma.

" 'What about Janey?' Ma asked.

" 'She'll have to stand it,' Pa said. 'It's not far now.'

"I waited a little, while they got ready to go. Then Pa made a motion for me to come on. I drew in my breath when I stepped down into the snow, it was so piercing cold to my bare feet. But I knew there wasn't any help for it. Pa was loaded down with all the meat we had, side meat, hams, and shoulders. And Ma was a-stumbling along underneath the huge feather bed and some quilts. We began climbing.

"It's only a mile up that piece, maybe less, and I reckon we were only about a half hour on the way. But it seemed to me like a hundred years. The cold was like knives a-stabbing into my feet and, in places where the snow had blown thin, the stones bruised 'em at every step. But I never said anything and I didn't cry.

"After a while we got up to this very spot, right where we are a-sitting now. Pa had built a lean-to while he was up here, a sort of house made of brush, with a roof and three sides. There was a pile of wood waiting to build a fire, and it wasn't long before we had one a-roaring, and it did seem like heaven. Though when I held my feet out to warm 'em they began to feel so bad that the tears came into my eyes no matter how hard I tried to keep 'em back.

" 'Take 'em away from the fire!' Ma said sharply. She got some snow and rubbed 'em and after a while they got warm and we had supper and we all felt happy. Pa sat on the ground facing the open side and looked out over those mountains that you see spread out down there. And though he never said much, you could see he felt like a king.

"He began to point about to this hillside and that one and to tell us what he'd plant on each one. He showed us where he'd build the house and the cow barn and where the spring was for getting water, and pretty soon I began to get the same feeling that he had, I guess. I forgot all about being poor folks—poor white trash as they used to call us down in the lowlands. Barefoot as I was, I began to feel like a princess in her own little kingdom!"

"Did you get some shoes right away, Granny?" asked Ellen.

"Oh, no, not for a long time. All during that winter I went barefoot. There was no leather for shoes and no money for getting any. But my feet hardened to the cold, more or less."

"But when did you get your shoes, Granny?" asked Mary.

"Well, I got some the next year, and in a way they came all through my own efforts. That sow that I'd taken such trouble for on the journey had a litter of pigs, and when they had grown big enough to sell Pa took one down to Asheville and traded it for a cowhide. Then he set out to make me a pair of shoes. He'd sit before the fire at night, after plowing corn all day, and cobble away. Before long I had some neat, strong shoes. They were a bit clumsy compared to those you

have on, Mary, and they didn't have any shine—rawhide shoes, they were—but I was proud of 'em, I can tell you that! I reckon there never was a pair of shoes more appreciated."

Granny broke off, distracted by sounds from the trail down below. "It must be your ma and pa a-laboring up the hill," she said, smiling.

The children peered downward toward the trail. Mummy and Daddy Calloway came into sight, groaning and perspiring. They hailed Granny.

"Such a climb!" exclaimed Mummy, wiping her face with her handkerchief. "My feet are killing me, just killing me!"

Ellen and Mary and Jody, still under the spell of Granny's story, glanced at each other shamefacedly. "I suppose that's the way we sounded when we came up," whispered Ellen.

"Yes," agreed Mary, pushing her shiny shoes back under the bench. "We'd ought to be ashamed, hadn't we?"